THE SIMPLE THINGS

BILL CONDON

pictures by BETH NORLING

First published in Australia in 2014 by Allen & Unwin

First published in Great Britain in 2014 by Allen & Unwin

Allen & Unwin – Australia
83 Alexander Street, Crows Nest, NSW 2065, Australia
Phone: (61 2) 8425 0100
Email: info@allenandunwin.com
Web: www.allenandunwin.com

Allen & Unwin – UK
c/o Murdoch Books, Erico House, 93–99 Upper Richmond Road,
London SW15 2TG, UK
Phone: 020 8785 5995
Email: info@murdochbooks.co.uk
Web: www.allenandunwin.com
Murdoch Books is a wholly owned division of Allen & Unwin Pty Ltd

A Cataloguing-in-Publication entry is available
from the National Library of Australia
(www.trove.nla.gov.au) and from the British Library

ISBN (AUS) 978 1 74331 724 2
ISBN (UK) 978 1 74336 315 7

Cover and text design by Sandra Nobes
Set in 11 pt Simoncini Garamond by Tou-Can Design
This book was printed in April 2015 at McPherson's Printing Group,
76 Nelson St, Maryborough, Victoria 3465, Australia.
www.mcphersonsprinting.com.au

3 5 7 9 10 8 6 4

The paper in this book is FSC® certified.
FSC® promotes environmentally responsible,
socially beneficial and economically viable
management of the world's forests.

To my friend Norman Smith, a kind and gentle man
with a great sense of humour

'Give your aunty a hug.'

I want to make Mum happy.

'Go ahead, Steve.'

I want Dad to be proud of me.

'Goodness me. He's not very keen, is he?'

And I don't want to make Aunty Lola feel bad. But I'm shy. You can't switch that off like a light. It's stuck on tight. I don't like hugging, except if it's Mum.

Mum's smile is only just hanging on. 'It's not because of you,' she tells Aunty Lola. 'Meeting new people is difficult for Stephen – isn't it, sweetie?'

'A bit.'

Dad mouths something that I can't quite make out.

Gopher?

Gopher goal?

'Huh?'

He steps closer and whispers. 'Go for gold.'

'Oh, right.'

'Let's forget it,' Aunty Lola says. 'It's clear the boy is having a hard time, and that's fine, because so am I. In fact, you'll have to excuse me – I have a terrible headache and I need to lie down.'

She puts on a scary face. Or it could be her normal face. I can't really tell. Then she stares at me as if she's trying to set me on fire with her eyes, before marching off. The march ends when Aunty Lola walks into her bedroom and slams the door.

'Oh dear,' Mum sighs. 'This isn't going to be easy.'

Ever since I can remember, at Christmas and on my birthday, Aunty Lola has sent me her love and ten dollars. She's really my great-aunt, but her Christmas and birthday cards always say *'Love from Aunty Lola'*. I've never met her before because she lives a long way from my home in the city. To me, the most real thing about her is that ten dollars. I always write back to say thanks, as soon as Mum reminds me. But I never send her any love. I don't want to lie. How can you love someone you don't know? You can't, not even for ten dollars, twice a year.

Now, after driving all day, we're here at her house. I sit with Mum and Dad on the back steps. In front of us is a small patch of knee-high grass and two rickety buildings, one small, one large. Beyond a sagging fence is a steep hill which leads down to mudflats and mangroves. Dad says there's a river out there at high tide. It doesn't look like one of those views you see on TV travel shows – the ones where the water's blue and there's yellow sand and sunshine. Uh-uh. I don't think anyone would come here for a holiday, unless they liked stinky mud. It's a freezing day, too. That makes everything worse.

'It must be pretty here when the water rolls in,' Mum says.

'Can we go back home?'

'We just got here, Stephen.'

'But I miss Blue.'

'Uncle Mike is looking after her. She's okay.'

'How about if we stay for another *whole* day, and then go?'

Mum folds her arms to keep warm.

'Why do you want to go home? It's nice here. You'll have fun.'

I look at the ground.

'Stephen?'

'Aunty Lola doesn't like me.'

'That's not true. You just got off to a bad start with her. She'll come around.'

'That's right, Steve. Don't take any notice of Lola. She's a grumpy old biddy.'

'John. Don't say that.'

'Well, okay, maybe that's a bit harsh. But she isn't the warmest person I've ever met.'

Mum looks at me. 'Lola can be sharp sometimes – a little bit snappy. But she's a good person, deep down. I saw a lot of her when I was growing up. She was happier then. Now she's got some aches and pains. That can make people cross. She doesn't like getting old. When she was young she rode horses and was a very good swimmer. She can't do those things now.'

I wouldn't like it if I couldn't swim any more.

'Does that help you understand how Aunty Lola must feel?'

'I suppose.'

'We're the only family she's got left.'

'Where are her family, Mum?'

'Her brothers and sisters died ages ago. The only one of their children who was close to her was my cousin, Molly. She's gone to live in England now, but before she left she rang me and we had a long talk. She said Aunty Lola hasn't been well – she had a fall and Molly had to take her to hospital. And now, with Molly gone, she's all alone.'

Dad takes over. 'So we thought it'd be a good plan to come out here and see how the old girl was doing. Make sure she's okay.'

Mum nods. 'It's our job to look after her. That's what families do.'

'Will we have to look after her for long?'

'Not really. We can only stay here till her birthday. That's three weeks from now. Then school goes back. And Dad and I have to start work again.'

'Three weeks!'

'It'll be gone in a flash, Stephen. And you might even like it here.'

I don't think so. It already feels like I've been here too long.

Dad knocks on Aunty Lola's door. Mum is beside him. I follow, a cup of tea on a saucer wobbling in my hand.

'Come in.'

The room is as dark as a cave. Aunty Lola lies on the bed. Her hair looked short before but now it's long and fluffed out on the pillow behind her head. Like a parachute.

'Here will do.' She clears a space on her bedside table. The tea splashes when I put it down.

'Sorry.'

'Too late to be sorry. It's done now.'

This is like when you meet a barking dog and you're not sure if it's going to bite you. Dad told me you can't let an angry dog know how scared you are. Or it'll attack for sure. You have to talk soft and walk up to it real slow. And watch its eyes.

'We'll let you spend some time together,' Mum says. 'So you can get to know each other.'

What? They're leaving? No! I can't watch her eyes on my own! I need help!

The door opens and Dad and Mum sneak out.

Somewhere in the darkness a clock ticks off the seconds. I silently count each one – five…fifteen… twenty-five.

Maybe Aunty Lola will go to sleep. Then I can sneak out, too. Thirty-five…forty-fi—

'So you're Stephen.'

Busted.

'Yes.'

'Well then. Tell me about yourself.'

'What kind of things do you want to know?'

'Whatever you'd like to tell me. Off you go.'

'Um…I sit next to Keysha Bennett at school.'

'Your girlfriend?'

'Nooo. I don't have a girlfriend.'

'But she's nice, is she?'

'I suppose. She's good at spelling. I'm okay but not great. I like handball. I'm not the best one. Liam is. He's one of my friends. The other one is Alister.'

'Only two friends?'

I nod.

'A small but select group, no doubt.'

'Right…we hang out a lot. Talking and stuff. Alister collects coins and Liam has a pet rat. I collect stamps and I like video games and dogs. But I don't like cats. They make me sneeze. Um…'

'Ran out of things to tell me, have you?'

'Almost.'

'Well, now you can ask me something if you like.'

'Okay.' There's only one thing I can think of. One important thing. 'How old are you?'

Aunty Lola's eyes open wide as an owl's. 'Why do you want to know that?'

'Because Mum said it was your birthday soon but she didn't say how old you'll be.'

'Your mother is respectful. A person's age is private.'

'But I don't know anyone who's really, *really* old. So I've got no one else to ask.'

Aunty Lola leans forward. I lean back.

'You say "really" far too often, Stephen. One "really" in a sentence is quite enough. Work on that, will you?'

'Okay.'

'Now, about my age. I don't suppose it matters all that much if you know. How old do you think I am?'

I put a hand under my chin and twitch my lips from side to side. Dad does the same thing when he's thinking.

'You don't have to say it to the very day.' Aunty Lola sighs. I can tell she's not very patient. 'Ten years either way will be good enough.'

'I think you could be about ninety. Around that. But not quite a hundred yet.'

She flashes those owl eyes again.

'You have no idea about age. Do you, Stephen? No idea at all.'

'Not really.'

'I'm about to turn eighty. If you must know.'

'What does it feel like?'

'Heavens above, you do like asking personal questions. It feels – oh, I don't know. Do you plan to be a detective when you grow up?'

'I don't know. I haven't really thought of that before. Dad says I might be a vet because I like dogs. But I don't like snakes. So if you had a sick snake I don't think I'd want to fix it. I like elephants, too… A detective might be a good job.'

Aunty Lola slides down in the bed and closes her eyes. This is my chance to get away.

'Are you asleep? You don't have to answer if you are.'

'I am not asleep.'

There goes my chance.

'Do you have another question?'

'What are your hobbies?'

'Being alone.'

'Aw. I'm going to have my own blog. When I see a movie, I'm going to write stuff about it. And I'm going to put in about music and books and if anything fun happens. And I'm going to have a comments part so people can write to me. You can write too, if you like.'

'Your *blog* will just have to get by without me. The world's gone mad with all this blogging rubbish. If I wish to write *stuff* about my life, I'll enter it in my diary. That's much more sensible. Don't you agree?'

Dad told me I should go along with whatever she says. That way I won't get into trouble.

'Yes.'

'Hmm. That's one thing in your favour. You say "yes", not "yeah". "Yes" is much better.'

'I've been practising. Mum doesn't like it when I say "yeah".'

'She's teaching you well. Keep up the good work.'

I nod again. Probably nodding is the safest thing to do with Aunty Lola.

'Lovely. Are we finished now?'

'I think so.'

'Stephen.' She reaches her hand across to me. Her fingers almost touch mine, but not quite. 'If I've sounded angry at all, I didn't mean it.' Her voice is softer. 'It's just that I'm not used to young people and their ways. I should be because I was around them for many years. I was a teacher.'

'Mum's a teacher, too.'

'Yes. I encouraged her to do it.'

'Mum's pretty smart. I bet you are, too, Aunty Lola.'

'Perhaps once. A long time ago. Now I'm out of touch. I get crotchety.'

'But Mum said you were good, deep down.'

'Did she? Well let me tell you, you have to go a very long, long way down to find the good bits – and they're few and far between.'

That's pretty much what I thought. But I don't tell her. I just give her a goodbye smile and turn to leave.

'One thing before you go.'

'Yes?'

'You look like the kind of boy who would be better at shaking hands than hugging. Is that true?'

'Um…'

Aunty Lola clicks her fingers.

'Well, is it true or not?'

'I'm still working it out.'

'I don't have all day. Hugging or shaking hands. Pick one.'

'Er...I usually only shake with Blue. Not with people. Blue's a cattle dog. So that's probably not counted as really shaking hands. Mum says I'm a good hugger. But I don't know if she's only saying that to be nice. Maybe you should ask her.'

Aunty Lola breathes out long and low, like a tired old dragon. She moves her hand away from me.

The clock becomes very loud again. Ten seconds...twenty...

Mum is waiting outside the bedroom.

'Did you have a good talk, Stephen?'

'It was okay. Aunty Lola is nearly eighty. Did you know that, Mum?'

'Yes, I knew that.'

'Does that mean she'll die soon?'

'Nooo! She'll be with us for a long time.'

'That's good.'

'So you like her, do you?'

'I'm not sure yet. Sometimes she's scary.'

'And she's probably not sure of you yet. Just be nice to her – that'll win her over.'

'Okay.'

The door opens and Aunty Lola wobbles out of her room. Now her hair is tied back again. That makes it easier to think of something nice to say.

'I reckon your hair looks better when it's long, Aunty Lola, like it was before. It's pretty.'

She raises her right eyebrow. That makes her left

eye close. I think I might be in trouble, because the eye that is open doesn't look very friendly.

'I've worn my hair this way for over sixty years,' she says. 'And I shall keep it this way.'

I look at the patterns on the carpet. Carpet patterns are as interesting as books, if you look really closely at them. It's better than looking at Aunty Lola. She's not very tall but her stare is huge.

'Come here, you.'

As I look up she waggles one finger in front of her face. I edge closer.

'It has been many years since anyone has called me "pretty". I never expected to hear it again.' She puts her hand on my shoulder. 'You're mistaken, of course, but thank you.' Then she turns away as if I'm not even there.

She's strange.

'I've prepared some sandwiches for lunch. We'll have them in the kitchen.'

Mum calls out to Dad. 'John – Johnny. Come and have lunch with us.'

'On my way, Rache.'

I follow Aunty Lola into the kitchen. She walks like she's on a boat, kind of rolling from side to side. One of her legs might be shorter than the other. Maybe she fell off a horse a long time ago, and hurt her leg. Or maybe that's just how old people walk. I'd ask her, but she might not want to talk about it. I'll get Dad to ask her later.

Once everyone is at the table it's as if the adults don't see me any more. Suits me. I'm happy just to eat.

The chicken sandwiches are the best. The meat is soft and it's white bread. Not that good-for-you kind that Mum always buys.

'It's so nice to see you again, Lola.' Mum takes a sandwich and passes the plate to Dad. 'It was ten years ago that we were here. Can you believe it?'

'Oh yes. I was sure you'd forgotten me.'

'We always meant to come back before this. But Stephen came along, and John's been busy with his work. And then I went back to teaching. Well, you know how it is. Time just gets away.'

'It does. But we make time for those we care about. Don't we?'

Mum looks at her sandwich. It's the same as me looking at carpet patterns, but not as interesting. Then she says...

'I'm really sorry that we've been so neglectful, Lola. But the main thing is, we're here now.'

'Yes, that's true.' Aunty Lola's face looks softer, happier. 'And I'm glad of it, Rachael. Very glad...but it's such a long trip for you.'

'You're not wrong.' Dad gets away with talking with his mouth full, but I'm not allowed. 'I was starting to think we'd never get here.'

'I enjoyed the trip,' Mum says. 'I know someone else who did, too.' She touches my hand. 'Didn't you, Stephen?'

'It was pretty good. We played lots of games.'

'Then I'm pleased.' Aunty Lola wipes her nose.

I don't think there was anything yucky poking out. Probably just itchy. 'But that doesn't change the fact that it was a marathon effort to get here. And there was no reason for you to come.'

'I think there was a very good reason,' Mum says. 'Your eightieth birthday's coming up. That's important.'

'No it isn't. I've had quite enough birthdays already.'

I slurp lemonade from a long, tall glass. Mum tops up her cup with hot water. It's a good time for me to check out the sandwiches. Most of the chicken ones are on the bottom of the pile.

'Lola,' Mum says.

'Hmm?'

'John and I were having a talk on the way up here…'

'And?'

'We both thought that it would be a good idea if – would you like to tell her, John?'

'No, no, you do the honours, Rache.'

Aunty Lola taps a spoon against her cup. 'Someone better tell me – and quickly. I can't guarantee I'll be around if you're going to turn this into a mini-series. I'm old.'

'Okay then,' Mum says. 'How would you feel about coming home with us when we leave? We'd love to look after you for a little while.'

'Ah.'

'Just for a holiday.'

'I see.'

'But if you liked it there, we'd be more than happy if you stayed. For as long as you wanted. It's warmer. Good for your arthritis. We're close to the beach.

There's nothing better than strolling along the sand, looking at the surf.'

Mum gives me her 'help me out here' look, so I do.

'I let Blue run on the beach sometimes, Aunty Lola. You can come with us. You don't have to go into the water if you don't want to.'

'Now there's an invitation too good to pass up,' Mum says. 'There are all sorts of activities you could do; groups you could join. I'm sure you'd soon have lots of friends.'

Aunty Lola holds a teacup to her lips, tilting it just enough so that she can drain the last of the tea. Then she stares into the empty cup, saying nothing.

Dad chimes in, to help Mum out.

'There's no need for you to answer now, of course. Just think it over for a while. No pressure. But, like Rache says, you'd be welcome.'

'I don't have to think it over.' Aunty Lola doesn't look at Mum or Dad. 'Thank you for the offer. But no thank you.'

Mum doesn't say anything. She looks sad. Aunty Lola nibbles at the edges of a sandwich, like a rabbit. The only noises I can hear are the squishy sounds of Dad chewing his food. And then there's a burp. From me. Sometimes I can make myself burp. Other times they just jump out. All by themselves. This one's a jumper. A noisy one.

'Stephen.'

'Sorry.'

'Lola. What about just for a week or two? I promise you'll enjoy it.'

'How can you promise that, Rachael? You don't know what I'll enjoy. The answer is no.'

'But—'

'This is my home. I've lived here all my life. I don't intend leaving until I'm carried out.'

'We only want to help you.'

'The best way to *help* me is by leaving me in peace. I'd much prefer that.'

'Molly told me you had a nasty fall and ended up in hospital.'

'I tripped. It was nothing.'

'Oh, right...Molly said it was to do with your blood pressure.'

I stack the sandwiches on top of each other, to see how high they'll go.

'Rachael dear, Molly's a lovely girl and I think the world of her but – what is that child up to?'

'Be careful, Stephen.'

'I am, Mum.'

A sandwich slips off the table.

'Lettuce and egg.' Aunty Lola peers down at it. 'I was looking forward to eating that. It was the last one, too.'

Jason Delaney's a real brain at my school. He reckons that when food hits the ground you have ten seconds to save it. After that it gets filled up with germs.

I throw myself onto the floor.

Aunty Lola curls her head under the table. 'What on earth are you doing?'

'Saving your sandwich.'

'Forget about the sandwich, Stephen.'

Mum probably doesn't know about the ten-second rule.

'It's all right, Mum. Most of it landed on Dad's shoe. So it's easy to get. Except for the pieces in his shoelaces.' I look up. 'Hi, Dad.'

'Hi, Steve.'

With at least a second to spare, I jump to my feet. In my cupped hands is the fallen egg and lettuce sandwich. It doesn't look quite as good as new. But I'm sure it has hardly any germs. To prove it I break off a piece and push it into my mouth.

'Yum! It still tastes good, Aunty Lola. You should try it.'

'Stephen.' Mum puts a hand over her eyes. As if she's ashamed. 'Don't you ever do that again.'

'But there's a ten-second rule.'

'I don't care.'

'Jason Delaney says—'

I stop talking when Mum gives me her special look, the one that shuts down all arguments. No one, no matter how big or strong, would ever dare go past that look.

No one except Aunty Lola.

She takes the sandwich from me and eats it.

'You're right, Stephen. It's very tasty. Thank you for saving it for me.'

'Glad you like it.'

Dad grins. Mum rolls her eyes. I bite into another sandwich.

Chapter 5

'How come your TV is so little and doesn't have colour, Aunty Lola?'

'I have no need for television. It's a waste of time. I watch the evening news. That's as much as I can stand.'

Huh? Who doesn't like TV?

'Have you got a computer?'

'Yes.'

'Can I use it?'

'No, you may not.'

'Aw.'

'My computer is not a toy. And it's always busy. I use it to research our family history.'

'That sounds like fun.'

'Fun?'

It looks like she's sniffing around the word. Like she's trying to work out what it means.

'I would hardly call it fun. It helps me remember the people that I knew. If I put them in my book, I keep them alive, in a way.' She squints at me, maybe trying to work out what I'm thinking – which isn't much. 'You don't understand, do you, Stephen?'

'I think so…sort of.'

'You'll understand one day, when you get older. Anyway, as well as researching our recent family, I find out about the lives of our ancestors from a hundred years ago. Sometimes longer. And then I write it all down in my family tree book. It's fascinating.'

'Am I in your book?'

'You are. So are your parents and your grandparents. And even their grandparents.'

'Do you put dogs in it?'

'It's a people book, not a dog book.'

'Aw.'

It's not what she says that makes me feel bad, it's the way she says it. Like she slams the words in my face. And now I feel her eyes digging into me. I try to think nice things about her in case she's reading my mind. It isn't easy.

'What is your dog's name? I've forgotten.'

'Blue.'

'Ah yes. I suppose it wouldn't hurt to have a dog featured in our history. If you send me a photo of Blue, I'll make an exception just for you, and put her in my book.'

'Really?'

'Of course *really.* I wouldn't have said it otherwise.'

Maybe she's not so bad.

'One other thing – I'm sorry you can't use my

computer, but if you wish to write a letter I'll give you a pen and paper.'

'Huh?'

'Stephen. Please. I'm not even sure that "huh" is a proper word. You must try harder to speak English. Just what do you mean by "huh"?'

'I don't want to write a letter. I just want to play games on your computer. Don't you?'

'Certainly not. And neither should you. It's nonsense. The same as that blogging business you talked about. I have two things to ask of you.'

'What are they?'

'Try not to use "huh" again – that's the first one.'

'That's going to be hard. I don't know if I can, but I'll try.'

'And number two – fill your head with ideas. Pour a book into your brain.'

'How can I do that?'

'Read! It's painless. You might even enjoy it.'

'I read now and then. But not much. I like comics.'

'That's a start. The more you read, the more your brain will grow.'

'I didn't know that.'

'It's a well-known fact. Albert Einstein was never without a book. Have you heard of him?'

'No.'

'The next time you go to the library, look him up. You do go to the library, I hope?'

'Alister likes going there. I go with him sometimes. They have a machine outside where you can get hot chocolate and chips.'

'Walk straight past that. Go directly to the books. Paper ones. Borrow some. Make reading a habit.'

'Okay…Can I read your family stuff?'

'My stuff?'

'The book about families.'

'I haven't shown my book to anyone. Besides, it would bore you.'

'No it wouldn't, Aunty Lola.'

'We'll see.'

Chapter 6

At home we have ducted heating. It's always set on 24 degrees. All Aunty Lola has is a one-bar, rusty heater. Everyone clusters around it like pieces of toast trying to get warm. But we're still cold.

'How about we buy you a new heater tomorrow, Lola?' Mum says. 'This one's just about had it.'

'If *you* want one, Rachael, go ahead. As for me, I'm happy to make do with what I have.'

'Don't you get cold at night?'

'If I start to feel chilly, I go to bed. It's no hardship. In fact, I might go now. It's been a long day. You know where everything is, don't you? The lights, the blankets?'

'I think so.'

'Well then, I'll see you in the morning.'

'Okay, Lola.'

For ages now, I've been practising some words in my head. Sometimes I do that when things are hard to say, like this is.

'Do you want that hug that you didn't get before, Aunty Lola?'

I said the words! Out loud!

'I beg your pardon?'

'Do you—'

'Yes, yes. I know what you said. I just don't understand it. I thought you didn't like hugging.'

'I don't really. But Dad says sometimes it's good to do the things you don't like. It makes you a better person. And I want to be better.'

'I see.'

'And there's another reason too – a really big one.'

'What is it, then?'

'You might die tonight and then I'd feel bad that I didn't hug you.'

Mum stares at me. 'Stephen, that's a terrible thing to say – even to think.'

'But that's what you say, Mum.'

'I do not.'

'Not about Aunty Lola. About Dad. You always hug him before he goes to work. And you kiss him, too. In case he gets killed in a car crash.'

'That's a little bit different.'

'Is it? Aw.'

'It's all right, Rachael.' Aunty Lola doesn't look angry. 'It's a nice thought.'

She crouches down and puts out her arms.

'Don't be all day. I can't stay in this position forever, you know. I'm not an acrobat.'

I lunge, wrapping my arms around her.

One potato. Two potato. Three potato. Four potato. Five p— that should be long enough.

'My, my. That was a hug and a half.' Aunty Lola squints at me, long and hard. As if she suspects me of being up to some terrible mischief. As if she thinks no one would ever want to hug her, and really mean it. It makes me wish I'd meant it more.

Before long it's time for everyone to go to bed. Mum makes me wear two pairs of everything, and she gives me an extra blanket. I don't feel cold any more.

'Remember, Stephen, if you need us we're just down the hallway.'

'He won't need us.' Dad gives me a secret wink. 'You're tough. Aren't you, champ?'

I'm not really.

'Yes, Dad.'

Mum puts a finger to her lips and then dabs me on the nose.

'Sleep tight.'

Click, click.

Nooo! The bedside lamp doesn't work. I was going to leave it on till I went to sleep. Only for this first night, not always. I don't worry about the dark when I sleep in my own room. Back home I've checked out all the shadows and murky corners. I know every sound and where it comes from. It's safe. But all that changes when I go to someplace new. It doesn't matter that Mum and Dad are close by. They're still too far away if I need them in a hurry. I used to like it when Mum read me stories to help me get to sleep. She hasn't done that for a long time now. Too old for stories. Sometimes I wish I wasn't. Anyway, there's nothing to be scared of. But I'm still not going to close my eyes, not tonight. I pull the blankets up around my chin and listen as the house squeaks and sways with the wind.

One potato. Two potato…

Early the next morning I go exploring with Dad. The grass in Aunty Lola's backyard is way past my ankles. Anything might be hiding in it and I'd never know until it got me.

'Are there snakes?'

'I don't think so, Steve. Too cold for them. But if there are any and they bite you, they'll die.'

'Very funny, Dad. Not.'

Still chuckling to himself, he bends down to tie his shoelaces. I can see the back of his head.

'Hey, Dad?'

'Yeah.'

'You know your bald patch?'

'No. I have no idea what you mean.'

'Yes you do.' He's just pretending he doesn't know it's there. 'You're more baldy than the last time I looked. It's spreading. I reckon in a few years you won't have any hair left.'

'Thanks a lot, Steve. You've made my day.'

'You can't help it if you're bald. It just means you're old.'

He stands again and looks at me, grinning. 'If I go bald, that means you will, too, mate. It's called heredity. Ha-ha!'

Me, bald? No way.

'Nice try, Dad. But you are so, so wrong.'

In front of us is a rusty barrel.

'Incinerator,' Dad says. 'You throw your junk in there and burn it.'

Close by is a shed. It looks like it's been there for a hundred years, easy. I look through the window. It's dark inside and I can't see anything.

'What's in there?'

'I think Lola uses it as some kind of office.' Dad stands with me at the window, a hand on my shoulder. 'She doesn't like people going inside. Mum told me.' He drops in close to my ear and whispers. 'There's a door in there – to another room. She *always* keeps it locked. No one goes into that room. Ever. Your mum remembers it being like that years ago, when she was about your age. Oh yeah, I'd like to know what she's got inside.'

'What do you think is in the secret room, Dad?'

'Could be anything. Treasure. Dead bodies.'

'No, really.'

'I have no idea. But I know it must be big-time for her to keep it locked up for so long.'

'Aunty Lola might tell me about it if I ask her.'

'Possibly. Or she might snaffle you up and push you in the room and then we'll never see you again.'

'You have to be serious, Dad.'

'Why?' He grins and gives me a pretend knockout punch on the jaw. Dad likes doing that. I like it, too.

We walk over to another shed. It's a lot smaller and tall and narrow.

'Second toilet,' Dad tells me.

'Why's it outside?'

'Years ago most people used to have an outside loo, just like this, Steve. You don't push a button to flush, you pull a chain.'

'Can I have a go?'

'Sure. But when you get in there, watch out for vampire rats.'

'Huh?'

'Vampire rats. Sometimes they live in backyard toilets. If they're hungry, they might try to eat you. Just thought I'd mention it.'

I'm used to his corny jokes so I don't groan.

'Dad. For a start, there are no vampires. That's only in the movies. And I've never heard of vampire rats. But even if that's a real name, they don't eat people.'

'You're absolutely sure?'

I nod.

'You don't think it's in any way possible that there's a rare species of rat with long pointy teeth?'

'No.'

'Huge hungry rats that hide in toilets and jump out and eat people? Especially boys.'

'No, Dad. You're making it up.'

'Suit yourself. Go in the toilet and have a look around. But if you get eaten, don't say I didn't warn you.'

Dad's kidding. I'm sure of it. I just wish he'd grin or laugh, instead of looking so serious. That serious look makes me feel a little edgy as I step inside the toilet. First thing I do is check behind the door. Nothing there. Thought so. The room is bare except for a roll of toilet paper, a book of crossword puzzles, a pen, and a calendar from last year. I try the chain. Pull down on it hard. Water gushes and gurgles. This is more fun than pushing buttons. And you can get muscles in your arms doing it, too. If you do it enough times. I don't have very big muscles yet but I'm—

Thump!

The door shakes. And so do I! (I wasn't expecting it.)

Thump!

'Yes?'

There's a growl and then, 'I'm hungry. Let me in.'

'I know it's you, Dad.'

'No it isn't. It's a talking vampire rat!'

'Daaaad.'

When I open the door Dad hasn't got his serious look any more. He can't stop laughing. But he didn't fool me. Not for a second.

'Can we go down to the water now?'

'Sure can, Steve.'

Dad lifts himself over the falling-down fence at the bottom of the garden. I follow him and we stand on the edge of the cliff that leads to the river.

'The tide's coming in now,' he says. 'Pretty soon the mud will be covered over. All you'll see is water.'

'When that happens, maybe we can go fishing?'

I copy Blue's hopeful look, the one she puts on when she wants to be taken for a walk. Or she's hoping for the leftovers from someone's plate.

'We'd need a boat out here, Steve.'

'Then let's get a boat.'

'I'll think about it.'

When Dad says that, he nearly always means *no.*

As we walk back to the house a voice calls, 'Hello there.' A tall man waves from the next yard.

We go over to him and I stand on the bottom rail of the fence so that I'm up almost as high as Dad.

'Hi,' Dad says. 'I'm John Kelly.'

The man's face looks like it's got sparkles on it. Dad's face gets like that, too. When he hasn't shaved for a few days.

'And this is my boy. Stephen.'

'Norm Smith.' He reaches over the fence to shake hands. 'Nice to meet you both.'

His hand feels soft. Dad's hands are rough because he's a builder and a bricklayer. Mum has soft hands…

'Are you a teacher, Mr Smith?'

'No, not me. I'm retired now, of course, but I used to be a cook. Not restaurants or fancy business like that. Basic food, that's me. I can do a real good hamburger. I'll make you one sometime, if you like.'

'That'd be good. I like hamburgers.'

Dad tells Mr Smith that his garden looks good. Like I said, Mr Smith is tall. But when Dad says that, he seems to get even taller!

'Why, thank you, John,' he says. 'It's not a great garden, but I get a lot of enjoyment out of it. Now over here I've put in cabbages. The caterpillars are a nuisance, but…'

Mr Smith sure likes talking about his garden. He's got a deep, rumbly voice and he smiles a lot. His hair is like Liam's brother's hair. It's tied up in the back with an elastic band. But Jonny is sixteen; so long hair is fairly normal for him. Mr Smith must be nearly as old as Aunty Lola. His long hair isn't normal. And neither is that headband.

'Mr Smith?'

'Yes, lad?'

'I like your headband.'

'You've got good taste. I like to call it a bandanna; that's more exciting than a plain old headband.'

'I like the colours. And the blue stars.'

'So do I. Lolly made it for me.'

'Who's Lolly?'

'Your aunty. That's what I call her.'

I take a closer look at the bandanna. It's way better than anything I could have made.

'She did a good job.'

'Yeah. Lolly's a clever woman. Generous, too. She reckoned the old one was ready to fall apart – like myself – so she whips me up a new one. And I love it.'

'I don't think you're going to fall apart.'

'Thanks, Stephen. Hope you're right.'

'Seems you know Lola pretty well,' says Dad.

'I do. We go back quite a few years. She's been a good neighbour. When she had her chooks she was always giving me eggs. I'd off-load tomatoes and broccoli to her when I had some. And we'd often have a cuppa together and a yarn over the back fence. Once in a while we'd go to the bowling club for lunch. Oh yes indeed, we enjoyed each other's company. But, you know how it is – nothing lasts forever.'

'Does that mean you're not friends any more, Mr Smith?'

He juts out his lips as he nods, and says, 'Afraid so.'

'Why not?'

'It's a long story.' He laughs, low and soft. 'Basically, I messed up. It was all my fault, no doubt about that.'

I want to ask what he did wrong, but Dad squeezes my hand. That means 'don't ask'.

'We better move along; things to do.' Dad looks at his watch, making sure Mr Smith sees him. Then he steps away from the fence. 'Good meeting you, Norm.'

'You too, John. And you, Stephen. If there's anything I can help you with while you're here, let me know.' Mr Smith's eyes become all sparkly. 'It's no trouble at all.'

'I'll keep that in mind,' Dad says.

He starts walking away, but I don't, because I know something he can help us with.

'Have you got a boat, Mr Smith? One that we can borrow so we can go fishing?'

Dad shakes his head. 'Steve, you can't ask people you've only just met to lend you things. Especially expensive things like boats.'

'It's no problem, John.' Mr Smith turns to me. 'But you're out of luck, old son. I don't own a boat. Wish I could've helped you.'

'That's okay. Is there a good fishing place around here? Where you don't need a boat?'

'There is, actually. At the bridge. I often go there to see what they're catching. There's hardly a day when they don't land a fish. Quite a tidy size, some of them.'

I *knew* Mr Smith could help us.

'Where's the bridge?'
'Down the end of the road and turn left. It's not far.'
'Can we go there, Dad? Now?'
'Mad about catching a fish, he is, Norm.'
'Can we, Dad?'
'Yes. We can go. Lead the way.'
'Thanks, Mr Smith!'
We start walking, with me dragging Dad's hand.

Five minutes exactly. Dad times it. I could do it in two or three if I ran.

It's a narrow wooden bridge, with peeling white paint. There are three grown-ups leaning over the rail, fishing with hand lines. Underneath the bridge some older kids are fishing. They stand on grey rocks, flat and round, near the edge of the water.

Dad walks up to a lady.

'Any fish yet?'

She wears raggedy jeans and no shoes. My feet get dirty sometimes, but not as dirty as hers.

'You come with me.' The lady waves her hand for Dad to follow her. 'See yourself.'

She takes the lid off a bucket. Inside are lots of silvery fish. Most of them are what Dad calls *tossbacks.* They're too little to eat so you toss them back in the water. Tiddlers is another word he uses for them. But one is so long it would hardly fit into Mum's frying pan.

The lady smiles. She only has a few teeth, but she doesn't seem to care who knows.

Dad frowns. That's to remind me it's rude to stare.

'You like what I catch?'

'Sure do.' Dad nods. 'Very good.'

I drop to my knees and stare between the rails into the river. The water's brown and dark.

Dad is beside me. 'See anything?'

'Not yet.'

Looking up, I see dark grey clouds steaming across the sky, like battleships. It's been cold all day, but all of a sudden it's super cold.

'I think it might be time to head home.' Dad turns up his coat collar so it covers his neck. I do the same. 'If we stay out here we'll freeze.'

'Just a little longer?'

'But it's going to rain, Steve.'

'We'll go as soon as it does. Okay?'

'No, we're going before that. I'll give you five minutes.'

Every five minutes doesn't feel the same. Like when there's only five minutes to the bell at school. And I'm busting to go to the toilet. That five minutes takes about a year. But when you want it to stretch out and keep going, five minutes runs away like five seconds.

'Time's up, Steve.'

'Aw.'

Something big flashes. Out of the water. Into the air. Just as quickly, it's gone.

'Did you see it, Dad?'

'I did, yeah. Could be a mullet. We might catch it one day. Right now we have to go. Let's move.'

We only take a few steps.

'Got one!'

My eyes zoom in on the teenagers below. One boy stands out from the rest; the one with long blond hair. The others say his name – Adam. He has a fish on the end of his line.

'Can we watch, Dad?'

'Okay. For a little while.'

Adam's line stretches and twists. But he seems so calm. So in control. His friends are just the opposite. They're like noisy fireworks, exploding with shouts. Adam ignores them and drags the fish closer and closer to the bank.

'Here he comes!'

Now I get a good look at the fish. It's all silver and squirming as it's hauled out of the water.

'Not bad,' Adam says.

He holds it up for the others to see, like a trophy. It's still struggling to get away. The other kids laugh. One of them has a knife. When he grabs the fish, I turn my head. I don't want to see what happens next.

'That's one of the best feelings,' Dad says. 'Catching a fish. When you get that first one – I tell you – that's really something. Brilliant.'

I just know it's going to be so good. I can hardly wait.

'It'll be your turn soon, Steve. Any day now you'll be hauling in your very first catch.'

'Hope you're right, Dad.'

'Oh it's going to happen. Believe it. It's exciting because the river is like a big lucky dip. You toss in your line and you take your chance. There are all kinds of bizarro creatures down there. You never know what you might pull up. Might even hook yourself a monster.'

As we walk home, I look around at the road ahead, and the trees and the gardens. I hear thunder boom, as if the world might be going to split apart. I see lightning rip across the sky. And soon I'm racing the rain, side-by-side with Dad. But all the time, every second of it, I'm still at the bridge. Over and over in my mind I watch that fish being caught. It isn't Adam who reels it in. It's me, Stephen Kelly. I'm on the flat rock jutting out over the water. I fight with the fish until my arms hurt. And when at last I win the battle, I hold it high for everyone to see. Just like Dad said, my very first fish is a monster.

Chapter 10

When I was a little kid I used to try to talk underwater in the bath. I knew kids who said they could do it, and I believed them. I swallowed an awful lot of water before I decided that it wasn't true. I still duck my head under the bath water, but now I keep my mouth closed. Sometimes, like today, I see how long I can stay down without taking a breath. It would be good to get a waterproof watch for Christmas…

'Stephen.'

Mum knocks on the bathroom door.

'Yep?'

'You're awfully quiet in there. You're not holding your breath, are you.'

'No.'

It isn't really a lie because I stopped doing it when she knocked.

'Because it's dangerous.'

'Okay.'

'Dad and I are going to the shops. Aunty Lola will be here if you need anything. Won't be long.'

'See ya, Mum.'

The front door opens and closes. Footsteps sound along the path. After a few minutes the car rattles into life and drives away.

I let the plug out of the bath and then block the drain with the palm of my hand. It almost feels like my skin is going to be ripped right off. Or as if something is trying to drag me down into the drain hole.

When I move my hand the water gurgles out, like it's saying, 'I'm free!' I block it again and it's my prisoner. Free, prisoner, free…

I know heaps of games like this. They're all fun. The only problem with this one is that, same as always, the water gets cold and I have to let it run away – till next time. I get out and dry myself. Flex my muscles in the mirror. Nothing's changed since the last time. Dad says it will. Muscles take forever to grow.

The house is empty. No Aunty Lola. I wander into the backyard. The grass is wet from the rain, but the sky is blue and clear, every trace of the storm washed away.

'Hellooo. Aunty Lola. Where are you?'

'In here.'

The toilet.

'What do you want, Stephen?'

I liked it before when I was in the toilet and Dad banged on the door and said he was a vampire rat. He didn't scare me or anything, but it was kinda funny. I don't think anyone plays tricks like that on Aunty Lola. I'm sure she'd like someone to…

'Did you hear me? I said, "what do you want?"'

'Nothing, Aunty Lola. I just didn't know where you were.'

'Well, now you do.'

'Right. I'll see you later. I'm going back to the house.'

'That's a good idea. Give me some privacy. Off you trot.'

But I don't go to the house. I creep up on the toilet, wrap both hands around the door handle, and hold it as tight as I can.

This is going to be sooo cool!

After a minute or so, the toilet flushes. Aunty Lola tries to open the door. It won't budge. I wonder why? Ha-ha!

'Oh bother. What a nuisance. Don't tell me I'm stuck here.'

She bashes on the door.

I'm not going to make a sound. Won't. Won't Wwww—

'Open up, you stupid door. Let me out!'

It's impossible not to giggle.

'Stephen. I heard that. What is going on?'

I clamp a hand across my mouth, while still holding the door handle with my other hand.

'What are you doing out there? Answer me. This instant.'

For three seconds more I hang onto the door handle.

Then I run.

Aunty Lola bursts out of the toilet. 'I see you! Stop! You little beast!'

I look back and see her hobbling after me. There's only one place to hide. The shed. This must be my lucky day. It's not locked. I duck inside and hide behind the door.

Now I hear footsteps. Louder and louder. And closer. It's a good thing that I practised holding my breath in the bath, because now I really need to do it. If Aunty Lola doesn't hear me breathing, she might not find me. I count off the seconds. A minute whooshes by. One minute and thirty seconds. It feels like my eyes are going to pop out of my head.

The door swings open. I gasp, and gulp a huge mouthful of air.

'What are you doing there, Stephen?'

'Nothing.'

'Doing nothing, is it? Ha! Out here. Right this minute.'

'Okay.'

Aunty Lola stands very close to me. 'Explain yourself.'

I can count every hair on her chin and not miss a single one.

'Why did you lock me in the toilet?'

'I was trying to be funny. I thought you'd laugh.'

'Then you were wrong. You were not funny. Not at all.'

'Aw.'

'I'm disappointed in you. Very disappointed.'

There was this one time I ate half a packet of chocolate wafer biscuits, all by myself. I ate them when Mum wasn't looking. We were in the supermarket. She hadn't even paid for them yet.

'Oh Stephen,' Mum said. 'I'm so disappointed in you.'

She looked at me as if I'd almost broken her heart. I'd forgotten how bad I felt that day. Now I remember.

I start to cry. I don't want to. Don't like doing it. Can't help it.

'Stop this nonsense. I won't have it.' Aunty Lola gives me a hanky. 'Dry your eyes. Right now.'

I use the hanky to blow my nose. It's dripping. My legs won't stop shaking. This is even worse than that time in the supermarket.

'I'm sorry.' Tears stream down my face. 'For shutting you in the toilet.'

'So you should be, horrible child you are.'

Now my bottom lip trembles. I bite down on it, but I can't make it stop.

'I'm really, really sorry.'

'Only one really per sentence. I told you about that. Have you forgotten?'

'Sorry.'

'And I've had quite enough of this *sorry* business, too.'

'Sorr—' I stop myself, just in time.

'It's over now.' Aunty Lola's voice is still sharp and pointy like a cactus, but not quite as much as before. 'We all make mistakes.'

'Even you, Aunty Lola?'

'Not as many as you.'

'But any?'

'Well, yes...I chased you, and called you names. I made you cry.'

'But I didn't cry very much. Did I?'

'Yes you did. Too much altogether.'

'I was trying not to.'

'If I were a nice person, you wouldn't have cried at all. But I am not nice and I don't expect I ever will be.'

'Aunty Lola?'

'What is it now?'

'Remember when I hugged you, and I said I was trying to be better?'

'Yes.'

'Well, maybe you'll get better, too. And then you'll be nice. All the time.'

'I doubt if I could be nice *all* the time. That sounds awfully hard...and boring.'

I nod, knowing she's right. Only dogs are nice all the time.

'But,' she says, 'perhaps I could manage it, just now and then. Only for you. No one else.'

'That would be good. And I'll help you, too.'

'Just don't go locking me in toilets any more – that's all the help I need from you.'

'I won't.'

'And no more tears. That's an order.'

'Okay.' I blow my nose one last time. 'Here's your hanky back. Thanks.'

She says I can keep it.

I take a look at all the things around me in the shed. First thing I see is the door leading to the secret room Dad talked about. I know that's what it is because there's a big padlock on the door. Aunty Lola sees me looking.

'What's in that room, Aunty Lola?'

'Nothing for you to concern yourself with. Or for anyone else. It's private.'

Dad was right. There must be something in there that's pretty special. I don't think Aunty Lola likes me even *looking* at the door. That's okay. There are lots of other things to explore; cups and medals and heaps of faded coloured ribbons.

'Did you win these when you rode horses, Aunty Lola?'

She nods.

There's horsey stuff everywhere. A cobwebby saddle lies on the bench. The walls are covered with horse pictures. The best one is a framed painting of a white horse, rearing up on its hind legs.

'That's a really nice horse, Aunty Lola.'

'He was.'

'What's his name?'

'Blazeabout.'

'Could he run fast?'

'Yes, he was fast and brave. I rode him over jumps in country shows. Blaze could fly. Or very nearly. He soared over the hurdles. I lost count of how many ribbons and cups we won.'

'What happened to him?'

'Oh, he went where all the good horses go.'

'Where's that?'

'He died.'

'How did—'

'You're wearing me out with your questions, Stephen. No more for a while.'

'All right.'

'Feel free to look around as much as you like. But don't touch anything. Unless I give you permission. Understood?'

'Understood.'

Aunty Lola takes a tissue and wipes dust from a frame. In it is an old picture of a girl with curly black hair. She keeps on looking at it – the way you do when you really like someone.

'Can I have one more question?'

'Since you asked so nicely…'

'Who's she?'

'Kathleen Julia. My sister and my best friend.

She had an accident when she was the same age as you.'

I have questions: What sort of accident? Was she hurt bad?

But Aunty Lola turns her back to me, like she's put up a wall that I'm not allowed to climb.

Now she sits at the bench, a large book opened in front of her.

'This is my life,' she tells me.

I want to say 'Huh?', but I know I'd get into trouble. Instead, I sit beside her and she turns the pages. It doesn't take me long to work out what I'm looking at. It's Aunty Lola's family book.

'That's my father…This is my mother.' She puts a finger beside the photo of each person.

'Who's that?'

'Another sister, Edith. She was your grandmother. It's a pity you never knew her. She was a very special person. They all were.'

I can't see anything special. To me they're only blurry, pale faces. Almost like ghosts. But Aunty Lola takes her time looking at every one of them. As if they're still alive, and looking back at her.

'This is me.'

In an old-fashioned black stroller is a chubby baby, sound asleep.

'Nooo. That's not you – is it?'

'It is.'

I study the photo up close. Aunty Lola sure has changed.

'Wasn't I a sweet child?'

'You were okay.'

'Is that the best you can come up with?'

'I think so. All babies look the same to me.'

'Stephen, allow me to give you a lesson in good manners.'

'Sure.'

'When someone shows you a baby photo – no matter what the child may look like – you are meant to say the baby looks cute. That keeps everyone happy.'

'You looked cute, Aunty Lola.'

'Too late. Far too late.'

She growls at me, like a lion whose tail I've stepped on. Then, once more, she flips through the pages.

Chapter 13

'That's Kathleen again.' Her eyes shine out of the small black-and-white photo.

'She died not long after that was taken.'

'Because of the accident?'

'Yes.'

That makes me feel sad, which is weird because it's just a photo. But she looks like a lot of girls at my school. I almost feel like I know her.

'Let's move on,' Aunty Lola says.

She turns the page, quickly.

'This was taken when I was a teacher.'

Her finger rests beside a lady standing tall and straight. Her hair has tight orange curls. And she's smiling. I look from the photo to Aunty Lola and back again.

'But she doesn't look anything like you.'

'It's me, all right. I was in my twenties then. We all change on the outside. You will, too. But on the inside we're much the same.'

'Does that mean that on the inside you're young?'

'Oh yes. On the inside I'm in my twenties.'

'Aw.'

'Or so I like to think.'

'Okay.'

'Our bodies get old and wrinkly, but we still believe in the same things when we get older.'

'What do you bel—'

'Telling the truth, being hard but fair…And twisting the noses of bratty boys who ask too many questions.'

I sway backwards, so my nose is out of reach.

'Any more questions?'

'Uh-uh.'

Another page is turned. This time I see cards with a red elastic band around them. Aunty Lola slips off the band and spreads the cards across the bench.

'Do you recognise these?' she asks.

'I don't think so.'

'You should. They're from you. I've kept all the cards you sent me.'

I open a Christmas card. I'd drawn a green Santa with blue ears.

'Yeah. I remember this one.'

'Thought you might.'

'My writing wasn't very good then.'

'It isn't a lot better now.'

'Aw.'

'Practice. That's all you need.' Aunty Lola drums her fingers on my back. 'Write to me more often. That will work wonders.'

'I'm not a good speller yet. But I think I will be.'

'One day.'

'Do you get lots of cards?'

'No. That's why yours are important to me.'

I only send her cards because Mum makes me. But when I get back home I'm going to send her a whole heap. Hope I don't forget.

'It's getting chilly in here.' Aunty Lola rubs her hands together. 'Let's go back to the house and get that heater going.'

I don't move, because, out of the corner of my eye, I see something interesting. It's a wooden box, with a lock on it. Old and mysterious. I want to pick it up. And rattle it.

Maybe it's full of money. Or treasure!

'You're dying to open that, aren't you, Stephen?'

'Is that all right?'

'Usually I'd tell you to keep your sticky fingers off it. But, since I'm making an effort to be nice…'

Please, please.

Aunty Lola glances at a key hanging from a nail. 'See if that fits. If it does, what's inside the box is yours.'

'Mine to keep?'

'Yes, but be quick about it, or I'll change my mind. You have ten seconds. One…'

I stretch as far as I can.

'Three.'

'You didn't say two!'

'Four.'

Now I stand on the tips of my toes.

'Five.'

And snatch the key.

'Six.'

I push it into the lock.

'Seven.'

It won't open!

'Eight.'

I'm desperate now. I try it around the other way.

'Nine.'

The key turns.

'It's open!'

'Too slow.' She grabs the box. 'Better luck next time.'

'But you didn't say ten.'

'Didn't I? That's easily fixed – ten.'

'Nooo. You can't do it like that, Aunty Lola. It's not fair.'

'It isn't? Why is that?'

'Because you went too fast. And you left out some numbers.'

Her eyes twinkle.

'Aunty Lola, are you making a joke?'

'I might be.'

'Are you?'

'Here you are.' She smiles and hands me the box. 'It's all yours, as I promised.'

'Thanks!'

'Go on. Open it.'

Carefully, slowly, I lift the lid.

'Cars!'

'You're not too old to play with model cars, are you?'

'Nuh. I've got heaps of them at home and I play all the time. Most of the ones I've got are plastic – but these are metal – almost like real cars! And I like all the colours, too. Look at this one – it's got fins!'

'They belonged to Joshua, my brother. You be sure to take care of them now.'

'I will, Aunty Lola, I will.'

I'm racing my cars under the kitchen table.

Vrrroooom! Screech!

Above me, Mum is trying to find out the names of Aunty Lola's friends. She wants to invite them to the birthday party.

Booooom!

Two of my cars crash. One of them blows up and I make the explosion noise.

'I'd like to help you, Rachael,' Aunty Lola says. 'However, as I've told you, I simply don't have any friends.'

'You must have *some*. Everybody does.'

'Not me. I've always been an outsider. I'm used to it now.'

A farm truck comes chug-chug-chugging along.

Behind it is a big square car with a long bonnet.

The driver toots the horn.

Beep-beep!

He yells to the truck driver:

'Get out of my way – you're too slow!'

Beep-beep!

The farm truck swerves to the side, almost bumping into Aunty Lola's foot.

I stare at the wormy blue lumps on her legs. Mum has ones like them, but not as big. They don't kill you or anything. They just hurt. Mum told me.

'What are you doing down there?'

'Racing cars, Aunty Lola.'

'Then play with care. I won't have you breaking them. If I see you being too rough, they'll be confiscated. You know what that means, don't you?'

'Yep. Sometimes kids in my class get stuff confiscated by the teacher. But she gives it back at the end of the day.'

Aunty Lola snorts. 'Well I'm not your teacher. I might give it back. And I might not.'

I drive my cars away, carefully.

'Now back to this birthday list,' Mum says. 'I need some names, Lola. What about Gladys Evans? You two used to get along well.'

'Heart attack. Went out like a light. That's the way I'd like to go. None of this hanging around.'

I take a wind-up racing car out of the box and scrape its wheels along the wooden floor. It goes real good.

Vrrroooom. Vrrroooom.

I let it charge.

Oh noooo!

It crashes into Aunty Lola's shoe.

'Oops! I didn't mean it!'

'Now listen here, boy. You're on your last warning.'

'I'm sorry.'

'So am I. If my toe is attacked again, all your cars – and your driver's licence – will be confiscated. Not for an hour. Not for a day. FOR EVER. Is that clear?'

'But I haven't got a driver's licence.'

'All the more reason why you shouldn't be running amuck on the road – bumping into innocent people like me! Don't you agree?'

I duck down very low and squeak, 'Yes.'

'It might be better if you play over there, Stephen.' Mum points to the hallway.

Soon the cars are lined up at their new starting line. Their engines are roaring. I'm good at making engine noises. On the other side of the room, Mum and Aunty Lola are still talking.

'Dorothy Thomas?'

'Thomson, her name was. In a nursing home. Mind's gone, poor thing.'

'What about that man you taught with? Percy someone?'

'Percy? I wouldn't know where to look for him. Perhaps the cemetery would be a good starting point. He was even older than me. I'd say he's left the planet.'

Mum keeps putting up names. Aunty Lola keeps knocking them down.

'This is terrible, Lola. I can't think of anyone to invite to your birthday party.'

'Then we'll hear no more of it. A good thing, too. You don't have parties at my age. You have funerals.'

'Lola! That's so negative.'

'I don't believe in running from the truth, Rachael. You face things head-on, that's what you do.'

It's interesting listening to grown-ups talk, but the sound of Dad's footsteps tramping down the hall interrupts.

'Hi, Dad.'

'Hiya.' As he turns to look at me he accidentally knocks some cars.

'Sorry, Steve.' He picks up a couple for a closer look. 'I haven't seen these before.'

'Aunty Lola gave them to me.'

'That's kind of her.'

'Will you play with me, Dad?'

'Don't know if I've got time right now.'

'Maybe later?'

'Yeah, maybe. I have to talk to Mum first – and Lola.'

Plenty of times I've thought about getting a number-two cut like Alister, but then Dad wouldn't be able to ruffle my hair as he goes past, like he does now. He strolls towards Mum and Aunty Lola, but pauses next to the phone.

'Phone's off the hook, Lola,' he says.

Aunty Lola nods. 'I know. That way I don't get disappointed when no one rings me.'

I don't get it, but Dad seems to. 'Fair enough,' he says. Then he changes the subject. 'Met your neighbour today – Norm. Seems like a nice fella.'

'He's someone we could invite,' Mum says. 'What do you say, Lola?'

'No. I don't think so.'

'He calls you Lolly,' I tell her.

Dad nods. 'Yeah, that's right. You made him that

headband he had on. Did a fine job, too. Fair bit of work went into that.'

Mum stares at Aunty Lola as if she's seeing a different person.

'What's this all about?' she asks.

Aunty Lola shrugs. 'It's a plain and simple headband, not a work of art. His old one was in a terrible state. It was a disgrace, so I made him a new one. That's all.'

'Tell me more. This is very interesting.'

'There's nothing to tell.' Aunty Lola shifts in her seat. 'He gave me vegetables from his garden. I thought it was only polite to repay him. Heavens, Rachael. It took me hardly any time to make the silly thing. Don't go on about it.'

'Aunty Lola?'

'Are you going to cross-examine me, too?'

I'm not sure how to answer, so all I do is open my mouth.

'Out with it, Stephen. What's your question?'

'Mr Smith said you used to give him eggs.'

'Only because they would have been wasted otherwise.'

'And you used to have lunch with him at the bowling club.'

'What of it? That was at least two years ago.'

'Sounds like you pair were an item,' Mum teases.

'Oh, poppycock.'

'Are you *sure* we can't invite him to the party?'

'Now look here.' Aunty Lola's eyes flash angrily. 'Norm and I had a friendship once, but we don't any more. It's over. Just like this conversation.'

Chapter 15

Dad is always the first one out of bed. He says he likes watching the day wake up. Most times back home, I don't hear him. But I do now. The squeaky door wakes me.

'What are you doing, Dad?'

'Waiting for the sun to show itself. It's quite a sight.'

'Can I wait with you?'

'Better not. It's too early. You should probably go back to bed.'

'But I'm wide awake. And I want to be with you. Can I, Dad?'

'No way. You're a nuisance.'

He tries to keep a straight face, but a grin breaks through.

'Daaad.'

'Steeeve.'

We both laugh.

'Course you can stay.'

We sit on the back steps. Dad has a rug over his legs, but when he sees me shiver, he puts it around my shoulders.

'That better?'

'Heaps.'

'Here you go.' He gives me his mug of hot chocolate. It's nearly full. 'This will get you even warmer.'

It's sweet and hot. I feel myself warming up with every mouthful.

'Hit the spot, Steve?'

'Bullseye!'

'Good.'

'Dad, I was thinking about Mr Smith.'

'What about him?'

'I like him. Do you?'

'Yeah, I s'pose.'

'How come Aunty Lola doesn't want to be his friend?'

'Don't know, Steve. You wouldn't need to do much to upset her. He might be better off without her.'

'Why?'

'Because she can be a cranky old thing; a bit stubborn, difficult. Don't you think?'

'She gave me a box full of cars.'

Dad grins. 'You're like your mum, you know that?'

'The way I look?'

'Nooo. You look like me – tall, dark and handsome.'

'But not bald – eh, Dad?'

'Watch it, mister.' He laughs as he says it. 'What I meant was, you find the good things in people, like Mum does. A lot of us don't even look. I want you to always keep looking. Will you do that?'

'No problem, Dad.'

'That's the way.' He squeezes my knee. 'How does that grab ya?'

'Oww!' I moan, pretending that I'm in agony.

'Shh. You'll wake Mum.'

I turn down my moan so only Dad can hear. 'Owww.'

We're both smiling as we gaze up into the clouds. There's nothing to see but dark, fantastic shapes – like a haunted house, only it's a haunted sky.

'Not long to go now, Steve. Then you'll see how the world wakes up.'

I haven't seen a sunrise before. I've wanted to, but it happens really early, when I'm sound asleep. It's hard to wake up in time.

'Will it be good, Dad?'

'It will. I used to do this with my own father. We'd ride our bikes down to the headland, plonk ourselves on the grass, and watch the sun come up. Same as we're doing now. Yeah. I loved every second of it. It's the simple things like this that stay with you, Steve. You reckon you'll remember today?'

'Think so, Dad.'

Two minutes go by. I time them. We hear the birds first. It's like they're in every tree, having their breakfast. Then the lights flicker on.

'Look.'

Streaks of bright yellow sky cut through the dark. Bit by bit we see the water come alive as the light falls on it. The mud is all gone.

'Keep watching, Steve.'

As the sky lightens we see the clouds. Red and pink and white and deep, deep blue. And then an orange ball bobs up out of nowhere, glowing and getting bigger…the sun.

'I've seen a few of those come up, Steve, but this one's special. You know what I'll remember about it the most?'

'No.'

'You.'

'Me?'

I think Dad is going to do a pretend head-butt, but he doesn't. He just nods.

Chapter 16

Toot, toot, toot.

'They're here!' Mum runs to the front door.

I watch from beside a window as three ladies get out of their cars. They were Mum's friends at school. Now they hug and kiss each other. I know what that means. I'll be next, unless I can get away. I could hide behind the lounge. Or maybe I could sneak out the back door without being seen. Or maybe I—

'Stephen. Stephen.'

I take cover behind the curtain, but I'm not quick enough. Mum waves to me. She must have some kind of GPS, because she nearly always knows exactly where I am.

'Come out here and say hello to my friends.'

I wish I could just shout 'hello' from here, but I know I can't.

'Coming, Mum.'

I reach Mum as she's showing her friends into the house.

'Hi!'

The ladies all say that at once. Then one of them says, 'He's a darling!'

This is torture!

Just in time, Dad wanders up to say hello. While he talks with Mum's friends, I take tiny steps backwards. Grown-ups always forget kids are around. Maybe I can still escape.

'Where are you going?' Mum says. 'Come back here.'

Then, before I can do a thing to stop her, one of the ladies makes her move. She walks straight up to me, kneels down, and hugs me.

Then she kisses me!

AAARRRGGGHH!

(I say that to myself.)

It's so bad, I can't even count potatoes. At least she doesn't get me on the mouth, but to be kissed anywhere on the face, by a lady who isn't Mum, is not good.

'What a sweetheart,' she says. 'Can I take him home with me?'

Without even thinking about it, or asking me or Dad, Mum says, 'Yes.'

WHAT?

NOOOOO!

'Oh, Stephen. Don't look so shocked.' Mum smoothes her hand across my face. 'I'm only kidding. I'm not giving you away to anyone. Ever.'

'What about me?' Dad asks. 'Are you going to give me away?'

'You?' Mum gives him a not-so-gentle shove. 'I'd give you away for sure, John. The only trouble is no one would have you.'

Mum and her friends have a belly laugh about that. I know they're only joking, but still, just so there can be no doubt about how I feel, I say, 'I'd have you, Dad.'

Early this morning Mum bought cakes. Now they're on the table. Pink and blue ones. Chocolate and cream. Yum.

Mum and her friends stand around, eating and talking.

Aunty Lola walks into the room and looks at the smiling faces. They're strangers to her, too.

'Mum's having a school reunion,' I tell her.

'Just a small one.' Mum smiles. 'We talked about it last night, Lola. Remember?'

'Yes, yes. Of course I remember.' She sits next to me and pulls a face that only I can see. I don't think she really remembers. And she doesn't look happy at all. I understand, Aunty Lola. You've lived alone for so long. In this sleepy old house. It must be hard to put up with an invasion of chattering ladies. It's hard for me, too. I wish that I could have stayed in my room. But I'm not allowed to do that any more when there are visitors.

'Now that you're older you have to make an effort to meet new people,' Dad told me a while back. 'If you don't, you might always be a shy boy.'

It's not fair. Mum and Dad aren't even the tiniest bit shy. How come I'm not like them?

'Stephen.' Aunty Lola touches my arm. 'I have a plan.'

I move my chair closer to her.

'Tell me.'

'Let's eat something,' she says. 'If we have our mouths full, we won't have to make silly conversation.'

'Good thinking, Aunty Lola.'

'I'm glad you approve. Now pass me a cake. A large one, please. And have one yourself.'

My cake is called a neenish tart. It's got chocolate icing on one half and vanilla on the other. Two bites and it's gone. Aunty Lola does the same with her cheesecake. She licks her lips, her eyes telling me it tastes awesome.

'Having a good time, Steve?'

I nod to Dad. I'm eating cake and I don't have to talk to anyone. How could it not be good?

The doorbell rings and Mum jumps up to answer it. That takes my attention from the cakes. For about one second. A vanilla slice is my next victim. Aunty Lola attacks a piece of lamington. We're like tag-team wrestlers, without the wrestling – just cake.

'We have a visitor.' I look up. Mum stands next to a girl. She's got straight brown hair and braces. They don't stop her from smiling.

'This is Allie,' Mum says. 'Mr Smith's grand-daughter.'

Allie looks at each face in turn. 'Hello,' she says, all bright and breezy. That one hello is for everyone to share. But Aunty Lola gets one all to herself. 'Hello, Miss Webster.'

'Nice to see you, Allie.'

'It's nice to see you, too...But Miss Webster?'

'Yes, dear?'

'The week is up. So can I have my soccer ball back? Please?'

'*Can* you have it back? Come now. You know better than that. We've been through this before. Many times.'

'Um...*may* I have it back?'

'That's much better. If I think of it, I'll throw it over the fence later today. But be warned, next time I might keep it for two weeks. Or more. And what happens if it comes over twice in one day?'

'It never comes back.'

'Quite right.'

Mum's friends look surprised. They can't take their eyes off Aunty Lola.

'Children need boundaries,' she explains. 'If a ball comes over my fence, it's an invasion. I don't care for invaders. Do you?'

The ladies don't know what to do or say. Mum thinks of something.

'Well now, Allie,' she says. 'You didn't just come over for your ball. You said you wanted to ask Stephen something?'

'Yeah.'

'Then go ahead.'

'Do you want to play, Stephen? In the park?'

'With you?'

She nods.

It's hard for me to decide. I don't usually play with anyone except Liam and Alister. And sometimes Keysha, if it's raining. She knows how to play lots of board games. I'd kind of like to play, but Aunty Lola might need me here so she's got someone to talk to. And the cakes are really—

'He'd love to play,' Aunty Lola says.

My mouth falls open. I was still deciding!

Aunty Lola points me towards the door, and pushes. 'Don't keep the young lady waiting.'

'Er – um – but...'

'Come on.' Allie has her hands on her hips. 'Let's go.'

'How old are you, Stephen?'

'Ten.'

'That's too bad. I'm nearly twelve...but I'll still play with you.'

'Thanks, Allie.'

'Can you do star jumps?'

'Probably, but I don't know how.'

'Watch.'

Allie bends down low, and then jumps up as high as she can. Then she makes a giant X by holding her arms and legs out wide, while she's still in the air. She does it three times.

'Your turn.'

I don't want to make a fool of myself.

'No, don't think so. I could do it – but my knee's sore.'

'You have to try. Go on.'

'What about my knee?'

'Just do one. That won't hurt you.'

Allie is hard to say no to.

I try.

'Not high enough, Stephen. Again.'

'But you said only one.'

'Yeah, but you only did half of one. Do a proper one this time.'

I try harder.

'Ha! Even my poppy could do a better star jump than that.'

'I told you I had a sore knee.'

'I don't think you have – I just think you're the worst star jumper ever.'

'Aw.'

'But that's okay. I still want to play with you. You tried – that was good.'

I feel bad about being the worst star jumper ever, but the look Allie gives me makes up for it. She's a good smiler. She sits on the grass and I do the same. We lean against the trunk of a tree, and she talks.

'I've got two sisters and a brother. They're older than me and they don't play very much. Hardly ever. They've got jobs. My mum and dad had a really big fight. That's why they don't live together any more. I had to choose which one of them to stay with. It had to be Mum. She needs me to cheer her up. That was a year ago so I'm used to it now. I still spend every second weekend with Dad. So it's all worked out real good.'

Allie makes it sound natural and easy, when it seems like just the opposite to me. If my parents split up it would be the worst thing I could think of. I would cry, for sure. And if I had to pick which one of them to live with, I couldn't do it. It would be a tie between Mum and Dad. I want them both. Always.

'Poppy told me about you.'

'Mr Smith?'

'Mm-hm. I live in Townsend Street. That's not far from his house, so I see him lots. Next to Mum and Dad, he's my best person. But he's sick. Mum said I have to be prepared. She thinks Poppy might die.'

Allie rips a piece of bark from the tree and stares at it. For a few seconds it feels like I'm out here alone, but then she flicks the bark away and looks at me. 'My problem is that Mum didn't say *how* to get prepared. And I don't know – do you?'

I wish I could help her, but I can't. 'Sorry, Allie. I don't know, either.'

'Yeah. It's not easy. I have to remember that he's lived a happy life. We talked about it and that's what he told me. I'm not to be sad, no matter what happens. Because that would make Poppy sad. And I don't want to do that.'

It's hard to believe that Mr Smith is going to die. He doesn't even look sick. And he smiles and laughs a lot. I think he's too alive to die.

'Hey.' Allie stands and brushes the grass off her pants. 'You want to have a race?'

'I suppose.'

'Okay. To the goal posts. But you're not allowed to start before I say "go". Got it?'

'Got it.'

Before I even get a chance to blink, Allie takes off, like a rocket. When she's halfway to the goal posts, she yells, 'Go! Go!'

I run like a rocket, too, but one with shorter legs. She beats me easy.

'Want to race back, Stephen?'

'All right. Only this time I'll be the one who says—'

Allie takes off. Just like before!

'Go! Go!' she roars, when she's too far in front for me to catch her.

This time I don't even bother to run.

'Tricked you, tricked you.'

'You didn't trick me.'

'Yes I did! You're so easy to trick!'

I stick my hands in my pockets and start to head back home. I talk to Allie in my head, telling her exactly how I feel. *I don't think I like you very much. You're a big cheater and a show-off. And I don't care if I never play with you again!*

I'm thinking all this bad stuff about her, when she says, 'I've made up my mind, Stephen.'

I turn around. 'About what?'

'About you.'

'Huh?'

'I like you.'

'Oh. How come?'

'Because you're funny. You make me laugh.'

This is strange. I try every day to make up funny jokes, but hardly anyone ever laughs at them. Now, at last I've been funny. I wish I knew how I did it.

'I have to go home now, Stephen. We can play again tomorrow. If you like.'

'All right.'

She grins, and runs off.

Chapter 18

Mum's visitors are still parked out the front when I get back from the park. Dad's on the roof.

'What are you doing, Dad?'

'Fixing loose tiles. But really – just between us – it's an excuse to get away. I wanted to let your mum and her friends have a natter. They haven't seen each other for years.'

'Can I come up and help you?'

'Nah. You should go inside. Lots of cakes left. You might even get a few more hugs and kisses if you're lucky.'

'Yuck! You sure I can't help you?'

He looks down at me, grinning. 'No, I'm almost finished. Maybe you could keep Lola company for a while. She's in her shed. Probably be glad to see you.'

'Thanks, Dad.'

I walk up the side passage to the backyard. There are cobwebs on the shed's window, but I can still make out Aunty Lola at her workbench. She's asleep. I tap the glass. Still asleep. Tap harder. She stirs and turns to me, then shakes her head. I'm walking away when the door opens.

'What do you want, Stephen?'

'I just came out to say hello.'

'Hello then.'

'Hello, Aunty Lola.'

'Is that all?'

'Er…'

'Dear oh dear.' She opens the door wider. 'Don't just stand there waiting for an invitation. It's never going to arrive. It got lost in the mail.'

'Huh?'

'Huh! Did you say "huh"? After I told you not to?'

'I forgot.'

'I'll let you off this time. But don't let it happen again. Come in.'

'Thanks…did you have a good sleep?'

'Sleep? What are you talking about? I don't sleep during the daytime. I was thinking.'

You were sleeping. I saw you. But I keep that thought to myself.

'I'm working on my family history book,' she says. 'I don't mind if you watch. But I don't want to hear a peep out of you.'

I pull a chair over next to her and watch as she writes in her book. Her pen is black and filled with ink. I haven't seen a pen like that before. Her face is just above the page as she writes, slowly and carefully.

'You write really good, Aunty Lola.'

'This? No. I used to have nice handwriting once, long ago. But it's scratchy now. Like a chook has run wild with a pen.'

'It's a lot better than my writing.'

'That's not saying much, Stephen. Your handwriting is…'

Aunty Lola stops. It's like she suddenly realises her words might be hurting me. They are a bit. I don't say anything, but she knows.

'Your handwriting is quite good,' she says, 'for your age.' She opens a drawer next to her and takes out a box of chocolates. 'Have one, Stephen. But none of this taking a bite and putting it back. If you don't like what you choose, it's too bad.'

'Thanks! Is there a piece of paper that says what's inside them?'

'No. You have to be daring and take a chance.'

'Because I don't like the nutty ones, or the ones that are really chewy. Sometimes they stick in my teeth. I like the dark peppermint ones. Are there any of those?'

'Oh for goodness sakes! You have one second to choose a chocolate.'

I grab one.

'Take two while you're at it.'

'Cool!'

'Now you eat those and I'll continue with my work. Eat slowly.'

One's a plain dark chocolate – no nuts, which is good. The other's strawberry cream. I don't like it so much, but it's not awful or anything. I eat as slowly as I can…

'Aunty Lola?'

'You shouldn't speak with your mouth full.'

'Dad does sometimes.'

'You just did it again!'

I chew, and swallow. Then I poke out my chocolate-coated tongue to show that my mouth is empty.

'That's ghastly. I don't wish to see what you had for breakfast.'

'Is it all right to talk now?'

'If you must.'

'Will you read me some of your family book?'

Aunty Lola lets her head drop onto the pages. She leaves it there for so long that I start to think something's wrong with her.

'Are you sick?'

She looks up. 'No, I am not sick. I am just trying to get some work done. It's very hard to do that when you're bothering me.'

'I didn't mean to bother you.' I get off the chair and trudge to the door.

'Back here.'

'But you said—'

'Oh Stephen, I don't mean half the things I say. You should know that by now. It's a habit I've fallen into so that people leave me alone. Not a very pleasant habit.'

'I can come back later.'

'No. I don't really want you to leave me alone. I believe you're growing on me.'

'Aw. That's good.'

'Not if you're growing on me like a wart.'

'Huh?'

'What did I tell you about using that poor excuse for a word?'

'Um...not to use it?'

'That's correct...I'll overlook it this time. Now, do you still want me to read to you from my book, or not?'

'Yes, please.'

'Then I shall. I wonder where I should start...'

'If you like, you can read it all.'

'There are thousands of words, Stephen.'

'I don't mind.'

'Let's try a small piece and see if you like it.'

'Okay.'

Aunty Lola reads.

'In 1826 Margaret Evans married Jacob Standish. She was eighteen and he was twenty-two. They lived in Newfoundland – that's in Canada, Stephen.'

I scratch my nose, then my ear. It's funny how when one part gets itchy, everything gets itchy...

'Margaret had nine children. Three others died during birth. Jacob worked as a—' Aunty Lola stops when she sees me yawning.

'I'm listening,' I say. 'It's really good. Will you read some more?'

'Yes, but not this. I know a better piece. One I think you might like a little bit more.'

Aunty Lola flicks through the pages. I try to get all of my yawns and itches out of the way before she reads again.

'Ah. Here we are. This is about your great-great-grandfather.'

'What was his name?'

'Long John Silverman.'

'That's a cool name.'

'He was a pirate.'

'Nooo. Was he?'

'Oh yes.'

'Do you have any photos of him?'

'He was around a long time before there were photos. But I'm sure you can imagine what he looked like. Go ahead.'

'Er...what do you want me to do?'

'Put a photo of Long John in your head.'

'How do I—'

'Use your imagination, Stephen. It's best if you close your eyes.'

'All right.'

'Now tell me what you see.'

'Nothing.'

'Squeeze that imagination. Go on. You can do it.'

'Um...he has a wooden leg.'

'Now you're getting the hang of it. Are there any termites in it?'

I open my eyes and grin.

'Eyes closed. And continue. What else can you see?'

'A sword. It's silver and it's got gold on the handle.'

'Very good. And?'

'He has a parrot on his shoulder.'

'Colour?'

'Green – and yellow.'

'What's this parrot doing?'

'Just sitting there.'

'Are you sure? What would a parrot do on a shoulder?'

'Um…I know! It's doing a poo!'

'Oh! You disgusting child!'

'It's green poo!'

'Horrible boy, you are. I am shocked!'

Aunty Lola's only pretending to be shocked. I can tell.

'This is fun!' I say.

'To you it may be. To me it is simply appalling. Now whenever I think of our pirate ancestor I'll have visions of…what you said.'

I laugh and laugh as Aunty Lola screws up her face. Like she's sniffing parrot poo!

'See, you didn't need a photo at all.' She pushes herself up from her chair. 'Your imagination is in good working order, Stephen.'

'Was Long John Silverman really a pirate? Or is he just a made-up story?'

Aunty Lola's back straightens. Her eyes bulge.

'A made-up story? Would I tell you a made-up story?'

I say 'No', but I think 'Yes'.

'I'm going into the house,' she says. 'So are you. Come along.'

'But I haven't told you my news yet.'

'Tell me on the way.'

I wait while she packs away her pen and her family history book, and switches off the light. Then she clicks the lock shut and closes the door.

We walk along the path that leads to the house.

'Go on then, Stephen, what's your news?'

'Allie told me that Mr Smith is sick.'

'Is he? I didn't know that.'

'Not just ordinary sick. Allie's mum told her she had to "be prepared", because he might die.'

'Oh…Are you sure you heard that correctly?'

'It's what Allie said.'

'I see.'

'Mr Smith is a nice man. I hope he feels better soon. Don't you, Aunty Lola?'

'Yes.' She nods slowly. 'I very much hope that.'

The next morning I help Dad pull weeds from the back garden. We've been doing it for nearly half an hour. Now I hear Mr Smith calling us. Allie is with him.

'I'm taking my favourite girl fishing at the bridge later on,' he says. 'Would you like to come with us?'

'It's tempting.' Dad rubs his bristly chin. For a second I think he might say yes. But then he says, 'I'd like to, but I've got lots of work on around the house. Maybe another time.'

'Can Stephen come with us?' Allie asks.

'Nah. He's got to help me. We'll be working here till dark. Maybe all through the night. Besides, he really doesn't like fishing. Do you, Steve?'

'I do so! You know that, Dad. I love it!'

He tries to look surprised, but his grin gets in the way. 'Of course he can go,' he tells Allie.

'Thanks, Dad!'

'But you'll need to buy a fishing line first.'

'We've got a spare one. Haven't we, Poppy?'

'We sure have, Al.'

I know Allie wants to run to the bridge as much as I do, but we can't leave Mr Smith behind. He walks almost as slow as Aunty Lola. Allie holds his hand and swings it up high as they stroll along. He's got one free hand but I don't know him well enough to take it.

Halfway to the end of the street Allie says, 'Are you fishing today, Poppy, or watching?'

'You know the answer to that one, Al. Nothing's changed.'

'Just checking…Poppy never goes fishing, Stephen. When he was young he used to hunt and shoot all the time. But then he shot this bird and—' She swings back around to Mr Smith. 'You should tell the story yourself, Poppy. I can't tell it as good as you.'

'Remind me later, Stephen,' he says.

It takes nearly fifteen minutes to reach the bridge. Allie times us with her watch. That's got to be a record for slowness.

'This is perfect,' Allie says when we see there's no one else here. 'More fish for us.'

We unpack our gear from the fishing basket Mr Smith has brought.

'I dug these up myself, Stephen.' Allie shows me the bait. 'They were in really gooey, oozy mud, but I washed them so they're good to go. Now we have to put them on the hooks.'

When I dream about catching a fish the hook is already baited. Having to do it myself is a lot harder.

'It's only a worm, Stephen. It won't bite you.'

I think worms should be called squirms. It's a much better name, and it describes them just right. I know this kid called Michael Foley who's got a worm farm. He says the worms in the farm are his pets. It's true! I'd much rather have Blue any day. She's never squirmy. Always soft and good to touch. I don't like worms very much, but I still feel sorry for them. It must hurt being stuck on a hook. Then they get thrown into the water. And sometimes a fish comes along and bites into them. It's not a happy life.

'Stephen, why are you taking so long?'

'I don't want to hurt it.'

Allie grabs the worm from me and pushes it onto the hook.

'There!' She passes it back. 'It didn't feel a thing.'

'How do you know?'

'I'm older than you. So I just know. Okay?'

I nod.

Older kids know more than younger kids. It's a rule. I can't wait till I'm older.

'Goodbye, worm.' I drop my line into the water.

Mr Smith looks up from the book he's reading. 'I know how you feel, Stephen. Next time I'll buy some prawns for bait. Frozen ones.'

We fish for an hour without getting a single nibble. I didn't know fishing took so long. First I think about worms and wonder if they can swim. Then I switch to thinking about fish, and catching them. I like eating fish that doesn't have bones. It's even better with hot chips and chicken salt. Maybe a couple of potato scallops, too. Suddenly I feel hungry.

'Is it time to eat yet?' I ask.

'Any time's a good time to eat, Stephen.' Mr Smith stands and points to a shop down the street. 'Food's okay there.'

We buy fish and chips and cans of drink. Dad gave me ten dollars for lunch but Mr Smith says, 'Keep it in your pocket.' He pays for everything.

After we wash our hands – mainly because of handling the worms – we sit down at a picnic table overlooking the water. I sprinkle vinegar over my chips. (The shop didn't have chicken salt.) I've never tried it before but Allie does it, so I copy her. Vinegar makes the chips taste pretty bad, but when I squirt on loads of tomato sauce they're good again.

'Remind Poppy, Stephen.'

'What about?'

'His bird story. He said you had to remind him.'

'Aw, okay. Will you tell me the story, Mr Smith?'

'It's not very exciting.'

'Tell him, Poppy. He'll like it.'

'All right then.'

Mr Smith takes a swig of drink. Then he starts…

'I used to be gun-crazy when I was a youngster. My brothers were the same. We all had rifles. I had three of them. Our dad would go out hunting with us on weekends.'

'Did you ever shoot anything?'

'My word I did. I'd kill an animal and it wouldn't bother me at all. But then there was this day when I was eighteen – sixty years ago. I saw a bird land on a branch. Amazing colours, it had. I didn't think twice. Took aim, squeezed the trigger – *Bang!* I walked up to where it fell and—'

'Wait till you hear this part, Stephen. It's spooky.'

I stop eating. And just listen.

'Well, before I fired, it was beautiful. Glorious. A moment later, as I stood over it, I saw all of its colour disappearing. It happened right in front of my eyes, Stephen. Its feathers became a washed-out, dirty grey colour. It was nothing but ugly. A piece of rubbish. And it was all because of what I'd done. I went home and broke up my guns and threw them away. Dad wasn't too impressed. My brothers thought I was mad. But I had to do it. And I've never killed anything since that day.'

'It's different with fish. Isn't it, Mr Smith?'

'I don't know, lad.'

'Oh, it's heaps different,' Allie says. 'Everyone catches fish, all the time. And fish are really stupid. If they get hooked, they don't even feel it.'

'Do you know that for sure, Allie?'

'Ye-ah. Everyone knows that. You told the story good, Poppy. Did you like it, Stephen?'

'Yes.'

We're all quiet for a little while, eating our lunch. Then Allie says that maybe we're using the wrong bait. Or we could try fishing further down the bridge, to change our luck. Mr Smith says the fish we're eating is cooked perfectly. He licks his fingers as he says it. All the time while they talk, and even as we walk back to the bridge, I can't stop thinking about that dead bird.

Soon we're fishing again. Well, really, you can't call it fishing if there are no fish in the water. I think they're somewhere else, and I don't blame them.

'If I was a fish I wouldn't go anywhere near water that was so close to a fish shop. Would you, Mr Smith?'

He laughs as soon as I say it. 'You're right there.' And, even though I didn't mean it to sound funny, he laughs some more.

'Shh!' Allie glares at me, not Mr Smith, even though he made more noise than I did. 'If the fish hear you talking, you'll scare them away.'

'Can I talk if I whisper?'

'No. All you can do is think.'

'What about?'

She shrugs. 'Up to you.'

Mr Smith coughs. Not just once. It's a cough that goes on and on.

'You okay, Poppy?'

He's hunched over, breathing hard and noisy. 'Nothing to worry about.' He clears his throat, and then straightens up again. 'Good as gold now. Must have swallowed a fly. Go back to your fishing, kids.'

Mr Smith reads his book. He doesn't notice me looking at him. His breathing is still all gaspy. I wonder if he's scared about dying. I would be. Allie's looking down at the water, but I reckon all that coughing has made her think about her poppy. Maybe she thinks about him all the time.

When I squeeze my eyes shut really hard I can see fish on ice at Con's seafood shop at the mall. Dad always ends up buying perch or salmon, but not before we've had a good look at all the other fish, just in case there's something better. Whatever fish I point to, Con knows what type it is. Now I can see all the fish from his shop. They're gliding by in the water below us. Yellowtail, whiting, trout, swordfish, flathead, perch, salmon. They've all got their heads on and they stare at me with their black eyes, probably wondering what kind of fish I—

'I've got a bite!'

Allie screams it.

'It's not a snag! It's a fish!'

Mr Smith stands up and looks over the side of the bridge. 'Reel it in, Al.'

'I am, Poppy!'

Her line isn't loose like mine. It's pulled tight. There's something strong on the other end. She really does have a fish.

Allie reels it out of the water. She groans when she sees it.

'It's only a can, Allie.'

'I know that!' She groans even louder.

'Never mind, Al,' says Mr Smith. 'At least you caught something.'

She takes the can off the hook and has a quick look inside. I have a longer look. Are those eyes in there?

'You better watch out, Allie.'

'What for?'

'I think it might have something in it.'

'Where?'

She holds the can close to her face, so she can have a better look.

'I don't think that's a good idea.'

'Why not? There's nothing – arrgh!'

Long red claws pop out. Then a head.

'Crab!'

Allie heaves the can back into the water. She shivers, and then hugs Mr Smith.

It's hilarious!

'Make him stop laughing, Poppy. Make him stop.'

'She's right,' Mr Smith says in a serious voice. 'You shouldn't laugh, Stephen.' He turns his face away from Allie, so she can't see his big, wide, happy grin.

It's raining, so Allie doesn't come over to play. Mum and Dad have gone out. That means it's only me and Aunty Lola together all day. I like being with her. She lets me help with her family history; cutting out newspaper stories and pasting them into the book. And she talks to me, like she hasn't done before – like I'm not a kid. I hear all about when she was a little girl, how strict her parents were, how there were lots of rules, and how she was always getting into trouble. Then – without me asking her to – she talks about her secret room.

'I have a case in there, Stephen. A very special case.'

'What's in it?'

'Some little bits of long ago. Precious things I can't bear to part with. They've been hidden away for sixty-three years. No one has seen them in all that time. I can't even look at them myself, because they're too sad – too many memories.'

'Sorry they make you sad.'

'I often tell myself: "I must do something about that silly old case of mine." I don't want people finding it after I'm gone, when I'm not here to explain what happened, how it was for me…I suppose one day it'll go into the fire. Soon, I think.'

'Will you show me what's in it, Aunty Lola? I promise I won't tell anyone.'

I expect to hear a big No, like a door slamming shut, but she thinks about it for a while, before saying, 'I'd like to, but I don't think I can.'

Aunty Lola stands on the front verandah and looks at the sky.

'It's fining up, Stephen. How would you like to come to bingo with me?'

'That would be great! What's bingo?'

'I'll explain on the way. The bus leaves in half an hour. Do you think you could be ready by then?'

'I'm ready right now!'

'Can I have the window seat?'

'You *may*.'

As the bus bumps along, Aunty Lola teaches me all about the game. I like that winners get prizes. Usually money. She says she'll give me half of anything she wins. 'Because tonight we're partners.' That is so good. But the most exciting thing will be when I get to call out BINGO, as loudly as I can. Like this –

'BINGO! BINGO!'

'That's enough, Stephen.'

'Did I do it right?'

'You did.'

'One more?'

'No. We'll get thrown off the bus. Keep it for the actual game.'

'What if I don't know when to say it?'

'You'll know. I'll make sure of it.'

At the bingo hall I head for the food table. There are pieces of cheese on crackers – not interested in them much – but I also see chocolate brownies and a plate of rocky road.

'Aunty Lola.' I tap her arm. 'You know what my favourite food is, in the whole world?'

'I do. You like rocky road. Your mother told me. But it's for after.'

'The brownies, too? They're my second favourite.'

'After. You've had your dinner.'

'Aw.'

'Stop thinking of all that sugary food. It's bad for your teeth.'

'Just thinking about it is bad?'

'Yes indeed. Now about bingo – you may sit with me. Or find yourself a nice secluded corner out of everyone's way and do some drawing. I brought pencils and paper for you. I think you'd like that much better, being all by yourself. But it's your choice.'

'Sit with you.'

'If that's what you wish. But no questions. You must be on your best behaviour. Bingo is a very serious matter.'

I reach into my pocket and pull out Dad's iPod. He let me have it, just for tonight. 'Is this allowed?'

'Stephen Kelly. Look around you. Do you see anyone else playing with whatever that foolish gadget is?'

'Not yet. But they might get them out later – if they get bored.'

'Give it to me.'

'But Dad said I could—'

'Now, please.'

I hand it over.

She drops it into her handbag and says, 'Confiscated.'

We have a few minutes before the games start, so I check out the hall. There are maybe seven or eight kids here with their parents or grandparents. Mostly it's old people. Some of them have really interesting faces. It's like when you look at a tree up close and you see all these twisty shapes and bumps in the bark. Mum says faces get that way from smiling and laughing for seventy or eighty years. Most of the people have grey hair. A few have hair that's totally white. Then there's blue hair, and heaps have no hair at all. (Dad might be like that one day.) I get up close and listen to them. There's a lot of talk about doctors and operations and a bit about people dying. But there's laughing, too. Loud, rocking laughing; the kind people do when they don't care about what anyone thinks. I don't get what's so funny, but I still feel happy. How weird is that?

Now I sit with Aunty Lola.

'Pay attention, Stephen.'

I concentrate as hard as I can. Mrs Smith is the bingo caller. Every time she says a number, she has a rhyme to go with it.

'Twenty-five: duck and dive.

Thirty-three: dirty knee.

Sixty-two: tickety-boo.

Fifty-two: Winnie the Pooh.'

I cover my mouth but a laugh still gets out. When people say poo it always makes me feel like I've been tickled.

'Shh!'

Heaps of people shush me, not just Aunty Lola. I mumble 'sorry' and go back to concentrating on the game. The players dab a pen over their cards, blotting out each number as it's called. It's the person who blots out all their numbers first who wins. I can tell when the game is nearly over because everything gets whispery. That's because people are listening really hard for their number to be called.

Aunty Lola taps my hand. 'Only two numbers to go.'

'Which ones?'

'Can't talk now.'

'Sixty-one: time for fun.'

'Was that your number?'

'No.'

'Forty-nine: rise and shine.'

'Was—'

'Yes. One more.'

'Sixty-six: clickety click.'

'Was—'

'No.'

'Four: knock at the door.'

'That one?'

'No. I'll tell you when.'

'Eighty-eight: all the eights.'

'Now, Stephen! Now!'

'What?'

'Say it!'

'Aw – BINGOOOO! BINGOOOO! BINGOOOO!'

'It looks like we have a winner,' says Mrs Smith.

I can feel everyone looking at me. I wish I could hide. I wish I could disappear.

'Up you go, Stephen. Mrs Smith is waiting.'

'I have to go out the front?'

'My word you do. So she can check your card. If it's correct, we win.'

'But—'

'Go on. Scoot.'

'If I have to…'

I keep my head down while the lady checks the card. That way I can pretend that I'm all alone; just me and the floorboards. It's not as good as disappearing completely, but it's close.

'All correct. We have a winner.'

'Good on you, Stephen!'

Aunty Lola says that. I didn't know she could get so loud.

'Here you are, sir.' Mrs Smith gives me an envelope – the prize. 'Well played.'

I rush back to my seat. Aunty Lola opens the envelope. There are four ten-dollar notes inside. She gives me two of them.

'Thanks!'

'What do you think you'll spend it on?'

I know without even thinking.

'Chocolates!'

'A splendid choice.'

'You can have half, Aunty Lola!'

'Chocolates are probably bad for me.'

'Aw, go on – we can have a chocolate feast!'

'Hmm. It's tempting.' She twitches her nose like a rabbit. 'All right then – a chocolate feast it is.'

A new game starts straight away. Aunty Lola gets down to just one number left. I'm on the edge of my seat, desperate to call out BINGO again. But someone beats me to it.

We play two more games. This time we don't even get close to winning. But the good thing is – it's time to eat!

'Here you are.' Aunty Lola passes me a paper plate. On it are chunks of rocky road and two brownies.

'Don't tell your mother I fed you all this rubbish.' She puts a finger over her lips. 'It's between you and me. And I'll have a small piece – so you won't have to eat it all yourself.'

'Deal!'

While we're eating, two ladies come over to talk. I back away, hoping they'll leave me alone. But Aunty Lola wiggles her finger in a 'get back here' kind of way.

'This is my grand-nephew, Stephen,' she says.

I have to shake hands with them, but that's all: no kissing or hugging – phew!

'There's no doubt you're related, Lola,' one of the ladies says.

The other one nods. 'Oh yes, a definite likeness there. And he's a fine-looking boy, too.'

Aunty Lola smiles a lot more than she usually does.

I remember a couple of years ago when we had show-and-tell at school. Jenny Tran brought a baby white rabbit to show everyone. This is almost the same. It's like I'm Aunty Lola's baby rabbit. I feel happy.

Chapter 22

Early the next morning the doorbell rings. Mum answers it.

'Can Stephen come out and play?'

'Stephennn. Allie's here.'

'We're playing cricket,' she says as we walk. 'That okay with you?'

'Yep.'

'I keep the bats at Poppy's house in case he wants to play with me. He used to once. Before he got sick.'

'He might play with us today.'

'Maybe.'

Mr Smith pours out two glasses of greeny-browny juice. Pushing a glass towards me he says, 'That'll put hairs on your chest. Down the hatch.'

'I'm not very thirsty, Mr Smith.'

'You won't really get hairs, Stephen, if that's what you're worried about. That's just something old people say.'

'I beg your pardon, Miss. What's this about old people?'

'Oh, I didn't mean you, Poppy. You're not old.'

I hold the glass up to the light. 'What are those floating bits?'

'Ginger,' Mr Smith says. 'It's also got mint and lime, carrot juice. Make a man out of you, it will.'

'Drink it,' says Allie. 'Or I'll never talk to you again.'

It's hard to decide. I could probably find someone else to talk to…

'Drink it!'

In three gulps I drain the whole glass. It tastes a little bit horrible, but not bad enough for me to throw up.

'I know something you don't know,' Allie says.

'What?'

'You don't get the hair on your chest. You get it in your ears!'

'Do not!'

'You'll find out – hairy ears!'

Dad and Allie would have a lot of fun together. They both make up corny jokes.

'Are you going to play cricket with us, Poppy?'

'I'd love to, Al. But I had my treatment yesterday.'

'What's your treatment, Mr Smith?'

'Boring stuff. I have to go to the hospital every week.'

'Poppy gets hooked up to a machine, to make him feel better.'

'What kind of machine?'

'It sucks out bad things, like cancer,' Allie says.

'Does it hurt, Mr Smith?'

'No, I'm used to it. Mostly it makes me tired. That's why I can't play cricket with you today. I don't think I'd be very good.'

'That doesn't matter,' Allie says. 'Stephen is *really* bad and I don't mind playing with him.'

My mouth falls open and I stare at her in amazement.

'Look, Poppy.' She laughs. 'Didn't I tell you he was funny?'

'He's a good lad, Al. I can tell that.'

Thanks, Mr Smith.

'But about the cricket.'

'Yes, Poppy?'

'I won't play. Don't think I'm up to it. But I'll come over to the park with you and watch. How's that?'

Allie hugs him.

'I'm batting first.'

'How come, Allie?'

'Girls *always* bat first. Everyone knows that.'

'Aw. Okay.'

Mr Smith settles himself into a seat under a shady tree. Then Allie gives him two jobs.

'You're the umpire, Poppy. And the crowd.'

'I'll do my best, Al.'

We find a garbage bin to use for a wicket. Allie stands in front of it and jabs her bat into the grass.

'Ready when you are, Stephen.'

My bowling isn't very good but everyone says my run-up is amazing. So I run back a long way and come steaming in like a champion racing car. And then I fling the ball down to Allie, fast as lightning. It goes wide. So does the second ball. And the third.

'Can't you see me?' Allie waves the bat in the air. 'I'm over here, not way over there!'

'It's a windy day,' I tell her. 'I think that's the problem.'

She laughs.

My next bowl is slower but straighter. Allie wallops it. After that, she does it again and again. Mr Smith claps and cheers her. He even cheers me when I chase after the balls. He's good at being a crowd.

When her score hits 20, Allie goes crazy. She jumps up and down, and shouts, and runs over to Mr Smith to hug him. It's like she thinks there's a million people watching and they all love her. Instead of only one.

'Give Stephen a turn now,' Mr Smith tells her.

Allie is a good sport. She hands me the bat without any arguments. She even smiles as I take it.

'Thanks, Allie.'

Under her breath, she says, 'Now you'll find out what real bowling is. I'm going to smash you!'

Well, she's nearly a good sport.

'Ready, Stephen?'

'Yep. And you can bowl as hard as you like.'

'You sure?'

'Bring it on.'

Batting is what I'm really good at. I'll show her who's best.

Allie's first bowl thumps into the bin.

Oh no.

'You're not out, Stephen. First ball doesn't count.'

Great! I forgot about that rule. It's a good one, because the first ball is always the trickiest one for me. But after that I'm okay. I think I'll beat Allie's score, easy. Maybe I'll get a hundred.

Oh noooo!

Her second ball thumps into the bin, too.

'YOU'RE OUT!!'

'I wasn't ready. Can't I have one more chance, Allie?'

'O U T spells goodbye. Seeya!'

I look over at Mr Smith, hoping he might help. He's gone to sleep.

'That's enough cricket.' Allie drops her bat. 'Let's climb that tree.'

Allie charges to it and reaches the top in seconds. I follow, but stay on the ground, looking up at her.

'Can't you do it, Stephen?'

'Yeah, but I don't want to.'

'Are you scared?'

'No.'

'What's wrong then?'

'I fell out of a tree once. That was the last time I climbed one.'

'How long ago?'

'When I was five.'

'Five!'

'It was my birthday, that's how I remember.'

'It's time you tried again. It's easy.'

'I think I'll stay here.'

'If you don't climb up with me, I'll come down and make you. And you won't like that.'

I think about waking Mr Smith. He might be on my side.

'Stephen, I'm coming down there on the count of three. One. Two and a half—'

I grab a branch and haul myself up. Just in time.

'That's the way. You're doing it.'

'Yuck.'

'What's the problem now?'

'A caterpillar. I almost touched it.'

'Caterpillars won't hurt you, Stephen.'

'It's a big green one.'

'Keep going!'

I move from branch to branch until I'm as high as Allie.

'I did it!'

Allie cups her hands around her mouth and yells, 'Yayyy!'

I do the same.

'Yayyy!'

The noise wakes up Mr Smith. He comes over to us.

'What's all this racket about, kids?'

'We're happy, Poppy. You've got to make a noise when you're happy.'

'Do you?' He scratches his head. 'Well then, I suppose I better make some noise too – 'cause I'm happy.'

Just like me and Allie he shouts, 'Yayyy!' And keeps on shouting as he goes back to his seat.

Both my grandfathers died before I was born, so I've never missed them. But now I kinda wish I'd known them. Especially if they were like Mr Smith.

'I'm sorry Aunty Lola isn't friends with your poppy any more,' I say to Allie. 'If he was I could see him all the time.'

'They probably won't ever be friends again, Stephen. Poppy did something bad. He told me all about it.'

'What was it?'

Even though the wind rises up, loud and wailing, Allie whispers it.

I go looking for Aunty Lola and find her in the shed. She sees me at the window.

'Door's not locked. Let yourself in.'

'Hello, Aunty Lola.'

She nods but doesn't look up. 'I've been doing some research on the computer. And I've made an exciting discovery.'

'What is it?'

'I've found one of your long-lost cousins, Stephen. Do you want to see him?'

'Sure.'

She waves me over to the computer, clicks the mouse, and up pops a photo of a gorilla.

I see a whole bunch of new lines on Aunty Lola's face as her grin spreads and spreads. I grin right back at her.

'I'm sorry, Stephen. He doesn't look at all like you…he must be related to your father.'

'I'm gunna tell Dad you said that!'

'Are you ticklish, Stephen?'

'No.'

I keep my arms pinned tight to my side.

'You are, aren't you?'

'No.'

'You tell your father on me and you know what's going to happen?'

'What?'

'This!'

She tickles me!

Aaarrgghh!

Help!

Heheheheheheheheeeeee!

'Are you going to tell?'

'Nooooo!'

'A wise decision, Stephen.'

It takes me a minute to get my breath back. Aunty Lola could give lessons in how to tickle. She's even better at it than Mum.

'How was your day?' she asks.

'Not bad. I played cricket with Allie. She's pretty good.'

'Quite an athletic girl, that one.'

'And I climbed a tree.'

'Did you now?'

'I know everyone climbs trees, Aunty Lola, but I fell out of one once and I wasn't going to do it again, but I did. I went to the very top. And it was windy, too.'

'That's an achievement. I'm proud of you.'

'Thanks...you know how you said I could talk about stuff with you?'

'Anything at all. Go on.'

'Well, Allie told me why you're not friends with Mr Smith any more.'

'Ah.'

'Because you got mad at him.'

'That's true.'

'But Allie said that was about two years ago, so I thought, maybe you've stopped being mad at him now.'

Aunty Lola fiddles with a button on her coat. Her finger circles it. She watches like it's a magic trick. Then, when the trick is over, she looks up at me.

'Stephen, the truth about Mr Smith is that he's a drinker. When he's had too much alcohol he becomes merry and wants to sing and dance. He also speaks far too loudly in public and says things that he has no memory of the next day. But I do. I remember every embarrassing word.'

'Allie said he doesn't drink any more, Aunty Lola.'

'The damage has already been done with me. After the last time, I told him he was no longer welcome in my home. There. So now you know. Is that what Allie told you?'

'Almost. The only other thing she said was that he asked you to marry him.'

'He did. And I told him he was a silly old goat. I knew it was only the drink talking. It's a hurtful thing to say something like that, when you don't mean it. It's a touchy subject with me because I heard it before, many years ago. He didn't mean it either.'

'Allie said Mr Smith's sorry – about everything. I know he still likes you, Aunty Lola. I heard him tell Dad.'

'Yes, yes. I'm sure all that's true. The problem is that I take a long time to make up my mind, and when I do, that's it. Over and done with. Mr Smith and I had our day and now it's gone. For all time.'

I nod as if I'm agreeing, but I'm not really. I reckon if they were good friends once, they can be again. I hope that's what happens.

Chapter 24

If there was a world record for breakfast-eating, I think I just beat it. An egg, cornflakes and a glass of orange juice, all gone before Dad even butters a slab of toast. Instead of eating, he reads the paper and talks with Mum. So annoying! To fill in the time I spin my knife on the plate. Tap my feet on the floor. And tell Aunty Lola – at the top of my voice so Dad can't miss hearing – that I've had my eyes open all night, thinking about going fishing today. Not just with Allie and Mr Smith, but with Dad, too!

'Up and at 'em, Steve.' At last he gets the message. 'Let's go catch us a fish.'

'Aren't you going to have your breakfast first, Dad?'

'Already had it, while you were asleep, mate. Didn't want to keep you waiting.'

Oh no! We could have been at the bridge by now! I think about head-butting the table, but it might hurt too much. All I do is groan.

Mr Smith has his fishing basket and Allie has a bright red bucket. She thinks we'll get a lot of fish today. I'll be happy if we only get one – and I catch it.

'Want to race to the corner?' Allie says.

'Only if my dad says "Go". That way you won't get a head start.'

'Fine by me.'

Dad holds a banana to his mouth, as if it's a microphone. 'Attention, starters: please take your places. I'll use this moment to remind patrons to turn off their mobile phones. And flash photography is not permitted during the event.'

'Daaad.'

'What?'

'You've got to do it proper. No fooling around.'

'This is the way it's done at the Olympic Games, Steve.'

'I don't think they use a banana.'

'They do when they have a power failure.'

'No they don't, Dad.'

He ignores me and talks into his banana again. 'On your marks. Ready…set…go!'

Allie is beside me. I'm puffing. I'm grunting. My heart is about to blow up. Wait. Wait. No. No! No! She's poking out her tongue! She's passing me!

'Come bacckkk, Allie!'

She doesn't.

'Thought you had her there,' Dad says, 'for the first couple of strides.'

'It's not fair.' I feel my shoulders slump. 'I never win.'

Allie pats me on the back. 'Don't feel bad. You'll beat me one day.'

'Do you think so?'

'Yeah. When I'm about a hundred.'

Dad and Mr Smith laugh. If I'd said that, I'm pretty sure it would be funny, but since I didn't, nah, it's not funny at all.

There are some people already at the bridge. The lady with only a few teeth is here. I don't recognise the two guys with fishing rods.

'Getting any bites?' Dad asks one of them.

'Not a one.'

'That's because the fish have been waiting just for us,' Allie tells me.

'Here you go, Stephen.' Mr Smith gives me a packet of frozen prawns. 'They'll be easier to put on the hook than worms.'

'Thanks for remembering.'

'Allie reminded me,' he says.

When I go to thank Allie she puts a finger in front of her lips and hisses, 'Shh!'

I let my line drop straight down, under the bridge. Dad walks further along to make sure we don't get tangled. Then he lets his line fall directly below him, the same as I did. Allie twirls hers around her head before letting it fly. It doesn't go out much further than mine, but she says, 'That's exactly where I was aiming.'

Mr Smith and Dad smile. They make sure Allie doesn't see them.

'Look at all the baby fish,' Allie whispers.

There's too many to count.

She tosses in a prawn and the babies swarm around, ripping off bits until it's all gone.

'That's a good sign, Steve.' Dad says this in his quietest voice. 'It means the fish are hungry. Today might be the day you catch one.'

I nod but don't say anything in case the fish hear me. They must have amazing hearing. When I'm underwater I can't hear a—

'Dad. Something just happened.'

My line goes tight, loose, tight. It jerks up and down like it's being pulled.

'I think you've got a fish, Steve.'

My hands are sweaty.

'Poppy! Poppy! Look!'

'Oh yes. I see. He's got one, all right. Looks like it's quite a size too, Stephen.'

I can't say any words. It feels like I've forgotten how to. I don't know what to do.

'Here, let me help you.' Dad puts his hands over mine. 'Reel it in. Like this.'

He shows me how to do it. And then he steps back.

'It's all yours now, Steve. You finish the job.'

The fish breaks free of the water, leaping high. It's red. It has wings.

The way Dad showed me, I reel it in.

'Don't let it get away!'

'You've almost got him. Keep going, Steve.'

I want to shut my eyes, but I can't.

'Nice and steady there, Stephen.'

Now I haul the fish out of the water. Up to the top of the bridge and over the rail. It flops about on the splintery beams like it's trying to stand on legs that it doesn't have. Allie holds it down with one hand and takes out the hook.

Its mouth is bleeding.

Dad and Allie and Mr Smith, they're all saying things to me. I can hear them. But their words are blurry.

I just keep looking at the fish and watching it struggle – and I know I've got to do something. I tip Allie's bucket on its side and push the fish into it.

Then I pick up the bucket and run. I know where I'm going. I know what to do.

Hang on, fish. Hang on.

'Steve?' Dad catches up and runs beside me. 'What are you doing, mate?'

'Have to get it into water. Can't let it die.'

'But—'

As I look into the bucket the fish flicks its tail. There isn't time to talk.

I run faster.

Chapter 25

I jam the plug into the bath and turn the cold water tap on as far as it will go. Mum and Dad are behind me, Aunty Lola too. They say things. To me they're sounds, not words. Their hands touch me. I can only think of one thing: the fish.

It's still flopping, but not as much as before. I splash some water on it. Maybe salty water would be better. I run into the pantry and get a packet of salt. Back to the bath. It's full enough now. I pour in the salt, and let the fish slide out of the bucket.

Swim. Please. Swim. Please. Please.

It doesn't swim. Not even for a second. It tilts over and drifts along on its side.

Dad lifts the fish up by its tail and slips it back into the bucket.

'Sorry, mate,' he says.

I walk from the bathroom to the hallway. Don't want to look at anyone or talk to them. I just keep going until I'm out the back door and onto the verandah.

I want to go home. I miss Blue.

The only place to sit is Aunty Lola's rocking chair.

I climb into it and think. Allie said fish don't feel anything, but I'm certain my one did. It was hurting. And it was all because of me.

'Is it all right if I sit with you, Stephen?'

I look up and see Aunty Lola.

'Okay.'

She pulls out another chair.

'I told your mum and dad that I should be the one to talk to you,' she says as she sits down. 'Because I'm experienced in these things and I know exactly what to say.'

'All right.'

She leans forward and softly says, 'But I told a fib. I have no idea what to say. I just wanted to be here with you.'

'It was only a fish,' I tell her. 'I know that's no big deal or anything, but it was my first one.'

'Shall I tell you what I think, Stephen?'

I nod.

'Then I'll be honest. It was a very curious thing that you did. In all my years I've never seen anything quite as peculiar.'

'Aw…'

'Curious, but very admirable.' She puts her arm over my shoulders. 'You must be a kind boy to care so much about a fish.'

'I don't think I'm all that kind. I just didn't want it to die.'

'Everything dies. That's how life works.'

'I know that, Aunty Lola. But it sucks.'

'I agree, Stephen. It's not a very satisfactory system…but it's all we have.'

Mr Smith and Allie walk onto the verandah.

'Hi, Miss Webster.'

'Hello, Allie.'

Mr Smith's face crinkles into a careful kind of smile – like he isn't sure if he should smile or not.

'Haven't seen you for a while, Lolly,' he says. 'You're looking well.'

Aunty Lola stares back, without a word.

So Mr Smith says, 'I hope you don't mind that I came over. I won't stay long.'

'As a matter of fact –' Aunty Lola sits up straight and folds her arms – 'I am rather surprised to see you. I thought we agreed that you wouldn't come here again. Didn't we?'

'That's about right. But I'm not here to see you, Lolly. I wanted to make sure everything was okay with the lad.'

'Stephen is doing quite nicely. Thank you for your concern.'

'Good, good. Well, that's all I wanted to know. We better toddle off, Al.'

'But we just got here, Poppy.'

He smiles at her like he's saying sorry, then takes her hand and starts to walk away.

'Wait.' Aunty Lola rubs her chin, to help her think things over. Then she says, 'I appreciate you looking out for Stephen, Norm.'

'It's the least I can do.'

'He told me you've been seriously ill.'

'Just old age catching up with me, Lolly.' He shrugs and smiles. 'But you know what they say, one day at a time. And today's brilliant.'

'I see...I'm sure it wasn't easy for you to come over here, Norm. As I recall, the last time you were here I chased you off with a broom, didn't I?'

'You did. That's one of the things I like about you, Lolly – you're full of surprises. A man never knows what to expect.'

'I'll take that as a compliment.'

'That's how I meant it.'

'Would you and Allie like to stay for a little while?'

'Yeah, I think we'd like that a lot.'

Mum and Dad join us and chairs are dragged together. Pretty soon the grown-ups are talking about gardens and the weather and cooking – boring stuff like that. It's as if they've forgotten all about me and the fish.

But Allie hasn't forgotten.

'I want to ask you a question, Stephen.'

She looks at me like I'm an alien who just stepped off a spaceship that's come from Mars.

'Okay.'

'Your dad said you put that fish in the bath. How come?'

'I don't know...I think I wanted to save its life.'

'That's nutty, Stephen.'

'Probably.'

'Sometimes when people catch a fish they kiss it, and then they throw it back. They're nutty, too. But no one ever puts a fish in a bath. Did you think it was going to swim?'

'I didn't think anything. I just did it. And I hoped.'

She stares at me like she's looking into my brain, trying to work out what's going on in there. I don't even know myself...

'Oh well,' she says, 'I suppose it's better to be a bit nutty than to be normal and boring.'

That cheers me up.

'Hey! Now you can have a fish funeral!'

'A what, Allie?'

'Have you still got the fish, Stephen, or did you throw it away?'

I turn around. 'What did you do with the fish, Dad?'

'Over there in the bucket.' He points to a spot near the toilet. 'I was going to dig a hole for it as soon as I got a chance.'

'Yes!' Allie punches the air. 'Poppy's real good at doing funerals. He did one for a goldfish of mine.'

'Don't forget your mouse,' Mr Smith says. 'I did that one, too.'

'Yeah!' Allie says. 'I almost forgot – Mum made chocolate crackles!'

It sounds like a party. That doesn't seem like a good idea, even though I love chocolate crackles. I think I want just Dad to be there with me when I bury the fish. He'll probably think of something good to say. He usually does.

I tell Allie I don't want her to help me with the funeral.

'Why not?'

'Just because.'

'Fair enough. But at least give your fish a name. You gotta do that.'

'I will.'

'Not a fish name like flathead or carp. A real name. I called my goldfish Lady Gaga. But you can't use that, it's taken. You have to pick a brand new one.'

Finding a name is easy.

'I'll call my fish Lola.'

Aunty Lola's eyebrows shoot way up.

'Are you saying I look like a fish?'

Dad stands behind her, nodding and mouthing *yes, yes.* For once, I ignore him.

'No, I'm not saying that, Aunty Lola. I thought it would make you happy. That's all.'

She looks at me long and hard. Then she says, 'Yes. It makes me happy.'

Allie elbows me. 'See? I knew it was a good idea!'

We go back inside the house and have drinks and biscuits. Mr Smith sits beside me.

'Been quite a day for you, Stephen.'

'S'pose.'

'Allie's keen on going fishing again tomorrow, but I told her you might want to give it a break.'

'Probably will. For a while.'

'I think that's a good move.'

'Mr Smith?'

'Hmm?'

'It wasn't the same as when you shot the bird. It didn't change colours or anything – the fish. I thought it might.'

'Birds and fish, Stephen. Different species. I'm no expert, but I doubt you'll get the same things happening.'

That makes sense to me.

Mr Smith stares past me, out the window. I look too. There's nothing there.

He turns back to me. 'I can only tell you one thing for sure, lad. I'll never forget that bird. Sometimes I just have to close my eyes and it's there. And I reckon you won't forget your fish. Not for many a long year.'

I tell him I won't forget. I don't tell him how sad I felt. He probably already knows.

As soon as Mr Smith and Allie go home, I ask Aunty Lola the question that's been on my mind all morning.

'Do you think you and Mr Smith are going to be friends again?'

'I doubt that very much.'

Before I can squeeze in another word, she points a finger at me.

'And I don't want you trying to talk me into it, either.'

'I won't, Aunty Lola.'

'You better not.'

'But instead of being proper friends, you could let Mr Smith come over for a cup of tea now and then. He'd like that.'

'Stephen, you're doing precisely what I told you not to do.'

'Am I?'

'You know very well you are.'

'Okay, but only because Mr Smith is really nice, and he—'

'Enough. You're a nuisance. I've been successfully shunning that man for two years and now you ask me to invite him into my home.'

Oh well. I tried.

'I won't say anything else, Aunty Lola.'

'There's no need to, because my mind is made up. And as I told you before, once I've made up my mind, that's it.'

I nod.

'Well, that's usually the case. However, a lady is permitted to change her mind. So, in this particular instance...I've decided I *will* ask him over for tea.'

'Yes!'

'Don't go congratulating yourself. It's not because of anything you said, Stephen. It's because he's unwell and if I can help him in any way, I should. It's the decent thing to do. But if I smell alcohol on his breath just once, I'll take the broom to him!'

'Thanks, Aunty Lola!'

She shoos me away and I run straight to Mum.

'Guess what? Aunty Lola wants to be friends with Mr Smith again! She just told me.'

Mum says, 'That's wonderful!'

I can't stop grinning.

Aunty Lola doesn't want a birthday party or any presents.

'Absolutely not,' she says. 'I'm too old for all that silliness. Next you'll be asking me if I want a jumping castle.'

'Cool!' I say. 'Can we have one?'

Mum frowns. I guess that's a *no*.

'What about just a small present?'

'No thank you, Rachael. I'm quite content with what I already have.'

'Here's an idea,' Dad says. 'Instead of a present, how about we repair a few odds and ends that are broken around the house? What do you say, Lola?'

'Very well.' She nods. 'Only minor jobs, though, you hear?'

Dad snaps an army salute. 'Minor jobs, it is. We're at your service.'

'You remember that, too.' Aunty Lola looks Dad up

and down like he's an annoying insect. 'I shall be very cross if my home is turned into a construction site.'

Dad bites his fingertips as if he's scared. He only does it as a joke for me, but Aunty Lola sees him. She shoots a monster glare at him. And now he looks really scared.

First we have to buy the materials we need from the hardware store. We also buy Aunty Lola a new heater. And I get to pick out which one. I like shopping with Mum and Dad. It's even better when we stop for an ice cream on the way home. Hokey pokey. It's my new favourite. After dark and creamy chocolates.

Back home again, we tackle the path first; pull off the old slabs and level the base with sand. I pour in water as Dad mixes cement. He says I'm a first-class apprentice. I don't say anything back, but it makes me feel proud.

Aunty Lola brings us some drinks while we're working. She watches while I help Dad smooth out the concrete for the new path.

'You're doing a great job,' Dad says. 'But I think you should get your hands dirty. We all should.'

Aunty Lola says, 'What are you talking about, John?'

'This.' He bends down and lightly scrapes his finger across the wet cement. 'Let's write our names on the path.'

'In my day,' Aunty Lola shakes her head, 'that was called vandalism.'

'Then be a vandal.' Dad's grin is big and broad. 'Go on. Just once.'

'Should I, Stephen?'

'Yes! Do it, Aunty Lola. Do it!'

'Oh dear,' she mutters.

'Rache.' Dad taps on the side window of the house.

'What's happening, John?'

'Wet cement. We can't let a chance like this go to waste.'

That's all he needs to say. We've done this before.

Soon Mum kneels beside Dad. She draws a big heart in the concrete. And they kiss. It's embarrassing.

'Must you?' Aunty Lola says. 'Really, it's too much. I'll have nightmares. And I expect Stephen feels the same – do you?'

I pull a face and poke out my tongue.

'My feelings exactly,' Aunty Lola says. 'I couldn't have put it better.'

Mum and Dad laugh. Then they write their names inside the heart.

'Your turn, Stephen,' Mum says. 'You too, Lola.'

I drop to my knees. Aunty Lola takes a step back.

'It's good fun.' I offer her my hand. 'We'll do it together.'

'I don't think so, Stephen. It's a long journey to the ground for someone my age. And then I'll have to think about getting back up. I'm afraid it's all too much trouble.'

'I'll help you.'

'We all will,' Mum says. 'It's a family tradition, Lola. It would be marvellous if you could be part of it. It'll only take a minute.'

'Will it wash off?'

'You bet,' says Dad. 'Eventually.'

'Eventually? How long is that?'

'A year or so.'

Aunty Lola opens her mouth very wide. Her eyes are wide, too.

'Dad's only kidding, Aunty Lola.'

'He better be.'

'Go on, Lola,' Dad says. 'I dare you.'

'No. No. No.' She gives her head a quick shake. 'That's decided me. I'm too old for dares. I should be inside – tucked up in bed with a hot water bottle and a book.'

'But Aunty Lola.'

'But what?'

'This is family history – like you put in your book.'

'It is nothing of the kind, Stephen. All it is, is finger-painting in cement. It's foolish.'

'But we're family, aren't we?'

'What is your point?'

'We're family and we're making history. See? Family history.'

Aunty Lola makes a noise. Kind of a sigh, kind of a groan. Then she says, 'Oh, very well. If I must. Tell me what I have to do.'

With Mum and Dad's help, she struggles down next to me and writes her name. I write mine, too. It's not very easy to read. The cement is hard to write in, and even on paper my writing isn't very good. But the smiley face I draw between me and Aunty Lola is perfect.

Next I help fix the stove. Aunty Lola says it hasn't worked properly for about a year.

Dad knows what the problem is. 'All we have to do is replace the broken elements. They're worn out.'

When we first came here I didn't think Aunty Lola liked Dad very much. It was the way she looked at him; her voice was all cold and angry. But now when she talks, I don't think that. It's like all the coldness has melted away.

'Once you've got it going again, John, I'll make some pancakes for us. I used to win prizes for them at the local show. That was a while ago, but I think I still remember how it's done.'

'Let's get cracking, Steve.' Dad starts unscrewing the lid of the stove. 'If we're scoring pancakes – prize-winning pancakes – then this job's our top priority.'

It only takes Dad half an hour – with my help.

'All finished, Lola.' He lights up every hotplate to prove it.

'What a good job you've done. Thank you so much.'

'No thanks needed.' Dad rubs his stomach. 'Just bring on those pancakes.'

'I'll get right onto it,' she says.

'What now, Dad?' I follow him outside to the front verandah. Mum's already there, watering pot plants.

'I'm going back up on the roof, Steve. Have to make sure all the tiles are in good shape so there are no leaks when it rains.'

'Can I come with you?'

'Yeah, you might as well.'

'Not so fast,' Mum says. 'Are you certain it's safe up there for him, John?'

'It probably is. Not too sure. But hey, it's not very far to fall.' He looks at me, grinning. 'It'll take more than that to hurt you, won't it, Steve?'

'Yep!'

Dad bumps me with his shoulder and I give it back to him – double.

'Ouch! I'll get you for that!'

He wraps me up in a bear hug and lifts me off my feet. 'Now for the body slam,' he says, laughing.

'John, I wish you'd take this seriously. I asked if it was safe.'

Mum says it loud enough for us to hear above our playing. She's leaning against the verandah wall and looking out at the garden, arms folded. She doesn't get cranky very often, but I think she is now.

'Steve.' Dad squats in front of me. 'Please tell Mum it's okay. Tell her I'd never let anything happen to you.'

'He wouldn't, Mum.'

'I know.' She looks at me, but not at Dad. 'I worry about you. I can't help it. Tell him that.'

'Rache.' Dad comes over. He stands behind Mum and rubs her shoulders. 'I'm glad you're careful about Steve. I wouldn't want it any other way. I promise to take good care of him.'

She rests her hand on his. For a second. Then she turns to me. 'And you take care of your father. Make sure he doesn't fall off the roof.'

'Okay, Mum.'

The ladder shakes when I climb it, even with Dad holding onto its sides. My legs shake a bit, too. I'm scared. But I try not to let it show on my face.

'That's the hard part over,' Dad says as I step onto the roof.

He climbs up and joins me. We walk around the edges and right to the top, checking for loose or broken tiles.

'Easy-peasy, Dad.'

Just as I say that, I step on a tile and break it. I think I might be in trouble, but I'm not.

'Doesn't matter,' Dad says, 'I was going to replace that one anyway. It's all good, Steve.'

When we see Mum at the clothesline, hanging out washing, I flap my arms like a bird. She shakes her head and looks away. Me and Dad chuckle to each other.

'It was heaps cool up there,' I tell Mum when we come down. 'You should try it. You can see all the way into town.'

'I'll take your word for it.' She pushes her finger down on my nose like she's pressing a doorbell. 'I think you should take a break soon, boys. I can smell Lola's pancakes. They're almost done, and knowing her, they'll be delicious. You better wash up now.'

'Give us ten more minutes, Rache. Steve's going to fix the back-door lock, aren't you mate?'

I hold up Dad's drill and press the trigger. It roars.

Mum's brow creases up, but only for a second. Then she smiles.

She walks to the kitchen, calling behind her, 'I'll expect you at the table in twenty minutes. No longer.'

Dad lets me drill in a screw. He puts his hand on top of mine and we both squeeze the trigger.

'Good job, Steve. I'll make a carpenter out of you yet.'

'Can I do another one?'

'Nah. I better do the rest. But you can help me, like this...'

My job is to hold the lock so it doesn't wobble when Dad drills the holes.

'You got it nice and tight, Steve?'

'Think so.'

'Are you sure? I don't want any wounded apprentices.'

'I'm sure. Go on, Dad.'

'Here we go then.' He squeezes the trigger.

'Johnnn!'

Dad turns off the drill.

'Johnnn!'

We run towards Mum's voice.

Aunty Lola is laying face-down on the kitchen floor. Mum is beside her.

'Holy hell,' Dad says.

'We need to get her on her side, John. Help me.'

They roll her over. Then Dad calls an ambulance. 'It's my wife's aunt,' he says into the phone. 'She's unconscious...yes, she's breathing. No, we don't know what happened.' He gives the address and hangs up. 'They're on their way, Rache.'

I ask if Aunty Lola's going to be all right. Mum and Dad don't answer.

Dad puts a wet cloth on her face. 'Lola.' He presses the words right into her ear. 'Can you hear me?'

Aunty Lola looks all around her, as if she doesn't know what's going on.

'I'm so glad you're back with us.' Mum is crying. 'There's an ambulance on the way.'

'I was making pancakes. I don't remember anything else. Did I have a fall?'

'We don't know,' Dad says. 'You were on the floor when we found you.'

'Hello, Aunty Lola.' I drop down next to her. 'I'm glad you woke up.'

'Thank you, Stephen...Rachael, did you say something about an ambulance?'

'Yes.'

'Oh Lord, no. I feel enough of a goose as it is. Call them up and tell them it's a mistake. I don't want to waste their time.'

'We can't do that.'

'Then *I'll* do it.' Aunty Lola tries to stand. She sways and almost loses her balance, then slumps back down. 'What is wrong with me?' she mutters.

The ambulance takes Aunty Lola to hospital. We follow in our car, but when we get there we're not allowed to see her.

'You might be here quite a long while,' the office lady tells Dad. 'We're short-staffed.'

The waiting room is nearly full. There's a TV on. It's a show about cooking. Not interested. We sit on hard plastic chairs. Mum tells me I can go out to the car and wait if I like. Dad says he'll come with me.

'No thanks. I want to stay here so I can see Aunty Lola when she's better. She is going to get better, isn't she?'

Mum says, 'I hope so.'

Dad goes to the office to ask about Aunty Lola. 'They can't tell us anything yet,' he says when he comes back.

Every time we see a doctor or a nurse I think they're bringing us some news. They walk past.

Hours go by. I wish I had a computer game to play. I go to sleep for a while, and wake up leaning against Dad. He said I snored. I don't think I did.

A nurse comes over to us. 'Miss Webster's family?'

'Yes.' Mum stands. 'How is she?'

'A lot better than when she came in. But still a little shaky. She'll need to stay here tonight, and possibly tomorrow. It depends on her condition.'

'Was it her heart?'

'At her age it could be a number of things. The doctors are still waiting on tests. We'll be able to tell you more when we have the results.'

'Is it okay for us to go in and see her now?'

'By all means.' The nurse smiles at Mum. 'She's sitting up and waiting for you.'

We walk down a long aisle with beds on each side. There are doctors and nurses dressed in whites and blues. Some of the patients have visitors and flowers. Some are alone. It smells bad in here.

Dad thinks so, too. I know because he sniffs the air and pulls a face. 'Chemicals,' he says.

I see Aunty Lola in a bed down at the end of the room, and I run to her. I'm not sure what I should do when I reach her. She decides for me.

'Give me a hug,' she says.

'Sure.' I do it and I don't even count off the seconds. Hugging still isn't much fun, but it's getting easier.

Mum kisses Aunty Lola on the cheek and says, 'Love you.' I should probably do the same…I will.

'Love you.'

No one hears me because it comes out in a baby whisper. But I still said it.

Dad straightens Aunty Lola's blankets, pulling them up to just under her chin.

'You had us worried there for a while, old girl,' he says.

'It happened so suddenly, John. I remember I was baking and then – nothing.'

'But you're all right now,' I tell her. 'The doctors won't let anything happen to you.'

'Look at this.' Aunty Lola shows me her hand. The top of it is dark blue; almost black. There's a bandage on it and a thin tube sticking out. The tube is hooked up to a machine beside her bed. 'I've had so many needles I feel like a pincushion,' she says.

'You're going to be fine,' Mum says. 'Isn't she, John?'

'Oh for sure, Lola. You're looking much better than you did when it happened. You must be feeling better, too?'

'I don't know what I'm feeling, John. I can tell you it's a shock being here. And I'm exhausted. I want to sleep. But I can't.'

'Should we go?' Dad asks. 'Let you have some rest?'

'I'm not leaving.' Mum strokes Aunty Lola's hair. 'I don't think she should be alone tonight.'

'I'll stay with you, Mum.'

'Nah, Steve.' Dad jangles the car keys. 'Your aunty could be here for ages yet. Best if I take you home.'

'Please can I stay?'

'Your father's right, Stephen.'

'But Mumm…'

'No buts. If I need you, I'll give you a call.'

'Hope you have a good night, Lola.' Dad pecks Aunty Lola's cheek. Then he gives me a gentle shove. 'Come on, mate. Let's hit the road.'

'Wait.' Aunty Lola holds up her hand. 'Seeing as Stephen can't stay, I'd like him to have a couple of minutes alone with me. Would that be all right?'

'That's a lovely idea,' Mum says. 'We'll come back in a little while.'

'On the bed, Stephen. Up nice and close.'

I shift closer.

'I'm glad you didn't mind staying with me.'

'I'd stay the whole night if Mum and Dad let me. I wouldn't go to sleep or anything. Not once.'

'That's kind. I wish I'd known you years ago.'

'So you could have fixed up my English and stuff?'

'No. Good English is not the only thing that matters.'

'Aw.'

'It would have been nice to watch you growing up. That's what I meant.'

'You still can! I've got heaps of growing up to do yet!'

'Yes, you have…' Aunty Lola's words trail away. She sighs like people do when they're sad.

'Is something wrong?' I ask her.

'No. Nothing's wrong…But I'd like to talk with you about something that's been on my mind. Would that be all right?'

'Yep.'

'For hours I've been lying here, thinking – what if I hadn't woken up when I fell down? What if it happens again?'

'Nothing's going to happen, Aunty Lola.'

'I know you're probably right – but if it does—'

She sits up in the bed and looks from side to side. No one else is close by except the lady asleep in the next bed.

'If it does, I wonder if I could ask you for a favour.'

'All right.'

'This is a very *big* favour, Stephen. You may need to think about it before you answer.'

'I'll do it, Aunty Lola. Whatever it is.'

'Sweet boy.'

I smile and shrug.

'Very well…do you remember that special case I told you about?'

'Your secret?'

'Yes. This favour is about that.'

'Uh-huh.'

'The keys for my shed and the room inside it are on a nail in the outside toilet – behind the calendar.'

'Right.'

'If I don't come home—'

'But you will.'

'You have to let me finish…If I don't come home from here, I want you to get the key from the toilet and go into my room.'

I nod.

'When you're alone, when no one sees you, take the case from the room and put it in the garbage bin. That's all. Will you do that for me, Stephen?'

'Yep.'

'*Yep* isn't enough. I need you to promise.'

'All right, Aunty Lola. I promise.'

I don't say a word all the way home. Dad notices.

'Thinking about your aunty, Steve?'

'A little bit.'

'What did she say to you back there – when you were alone with her?'

She told me I couldn't tell anyone. Not Dad. Not Mum. No one.

'Nothing much. She was tired, so we didn't talk for long.'

'Try not to worry about her. She'll get through this.'

'Are you just saying that, Dad? To make me feel better?'

'No, I believe it. The doctors will look after her. But…'

'What?'

'You have to remember that she's eighty years old. No matter what happens, she's had a long and happy life. That's as much as anyone can hope for.'

As soon as we get back home, I go to bed. I'm not tired, but bed's a good place for thinking.

'See you in the morning, Steve.'

There's a rewind button in my head. I only press it once – thinking about things – but then it plays and plays and I can't stop it.

Just remember that she's eighty years old

Everything dies

I need you to promise

If I don't come home

The locked room…the keys

I hear Mum crying. She's in the lounge room with Dad and he's hugging her.

'Did something happen to Aunty Lola?'

They don't answer. They don't see me. But I know. I know she's dead.

In the outside toilet I lift up the calendar. There are two keys on a nail. The grass is wet with dew as I walk to the shed. The only neighbour who might be able to see me is Mr Smith. His back door is shut and the curtains are closed. It's safe.

I unlock the shed. Now I stand outside Aunty Lola's room, the smaller key in my hand. It won't fit in the lock. My hands are sweaty. I try it the other way around, and the other and the other and – it turns.

Have to stop and listen, make sure I'm really alone. Don't hear anything. But I can feel my heart. It's thumping. Like it's trying to knock a hole in me.

Inside the room there's only one thing. On the floor, in a corner, is the case. It's big and wooden with gold hinges and it's so heavy I can hardly lift it.

But I do.

I'll keep my promise, Aunty Lola.

I hear the garbage truck rumbling down the street. I have to get the case out to the bin in time. I carry it to the side of the house and then drag it along the path. No one sees me. I make it out of the front gate and open the bin. But it's full right up! The truck is coming closer. I put my hands into the bin to push down the rubbish but underneath some cardboard on top, it's all bricks and concrete. I can't move it. I can't get the case in. I yell out to the truck driver, 'Help me! Help me!'

He drives straight past.

'Stephen.'

'I'm sorry! I really, really tried but it wouldn't—'

'Stephen.'

Someone is shaking me. I open my eyes and see Mum – with Aunty Lola! It's really her – she's not dead!

'It's all right,' Mum says. 'We're here with you.'

Aunty Lola sits on my bed. 'Oh, dear me. A bad dream and now all these tears. Whatever upset you, it's over now.'

'Are you still sick, Aunty Lola?'

'Not really. I've got pills to take and more tests to have. But that's for another day. Right now I'm only sick about any worry that I might have caused you. Because of what I asked you to do. I'm so sorry.'

'You're okay, Aunty Lola. That's all that matters.'

'Is this a private thing?' Mum says. 'Or can you tell me about it?'

'It *has* been a private thing for so long.' Aunty Lola clutches onto Mum's hand. 'But I don't want it to be that way any longer.'

Aunty Lola wets her lips. She takes a deep breath through her nose. And then she shares the secret with Mum.

'I have a case that's full of keepsakes, Rachael. I've had it locked away for most of my life. I've always prided myself on being the sensible one. But last night I was frightened. I wasn't sure I'd get through the night and I panicked. All I could think of was that I had to free myself of that case…so I asked Stephen to do it for me.'

'I was going to toss it in the garbage, Mum, but only if something happened to Aunty Lola. I'm glad I didn't have to.'

'Is that why you were so determined to come home from hospital, Lola? Because of this case?'

'That's right. I wanted to deal with it myself. And leave Stephen out of it. I should never have asked him. But at the time, I felt he was the only one I could turn to…'

A single tear runs down Aunty Lola's face.

Mum hugs her. 'I don't want you worrying any more. I'll help you get rid of the case, if you still want to.'

'I do.'

'Good. Let's get it done right now.'

'I can help, too – if that's all right, Aunty Lola?'

'Of course it is, Stephen. I couldn't do it without you.'

The room is much bigger than it was in my dream. I see a green lounge, shelves with books, a rack of dresses, some shoes. And on a table, in between two stacks of newspapers, is the case. It's brown and old-looking. No chain or lock. Just a worn-out belt tied around it.

'I know it doesn't look very important.' Aunty Lola starts to undo it. 'But there's so much of my life in here.'

She pulls on the belt but it's cracked and hard. It doesn't move.

'Let me try,' Mum says.

'If you can't do it, I will, Mum.'

'Thanks, Stephen, but –' she uses both hands – 'I think I've…got it!'

The belt snaps.

All Aunty Lola has to do is open the lid, but she just stares at the case. And now there are *lots* of tears rolling down her face.

Mum says, 'We'll go away and let you have some privacy, if you like.'

'No, no. I'm being a sentimental old duffer, that's all. We shall press on.'

She lifts the lid.

Baby clothes.

Aunty Lola picks up a tiny pink jacket and presses it to her face.

'It's amazing. The same feeling is still there, inside me. This brings it all back so clearly.'

She opens a plastic folder and takes out a black-and-white photo, the size of her hand. I don't know what to say, but Mum does.

'Who are we looking at?'

'My baby.'

'I didn't know you had a baby, Aunty Lola.'

'Oh yes. She was beautiful and perfect. But I couldn't keep her…these things happen.'

'She's got your eyes.' Mum nods at the photo. 'And you're right, she was beautiful.'

'How come you couldn't keep her?'

'Maybe Aunty Lola doesn't want to talk about it.'

'It's all right, Rachael. I want him to understand… the plain truth is I wasn't married, Stephen. This was in 1951. Back then, if you had children when you weren't married, it was thought to be a shameful thing. My parents decided that the baby must be adopted. I was seventeen. Not strong enough to fight them.

There's many a time I wish I had been. But there you are – that's what happened.'

'What's the baby's name?'

'The family who adopted her would have chosen their own name for her. I don't know what that is. To me, though, she will always be Kathleen Julia. I named her after my dear sister.'

'The one you told me about – who had an accident?'

'Yes. She drowned when she was ten.'

Mum looks out the window. 'It's raining. A passing shower, that's all. It won't last long.'

Aunty Lola eases herself down on the lounge. 'Is there anything else you'd like to know, Stephen?'

'How many questions am I allowed? Because I've got about a million.'

'Oh dear, that's just a few too many. You may ask two more, and then the matter is closed.'

'Okay – how come you didn't get married?'

'Well…my young man was handsome and kind. His name was Martin. I still have some of his letters in my case. I loved him. Very much. We talked about marriage. I certainly wanted to do it. But we were so very young…and since this is the day to be honest, I have to admit that he didn't really love me.'

'He must have had rocks in his head,' Mum says.

Aunty Lola smiles, just a little bit.

'Am I allowed a question, Lola?'

'Of course, Rachael.'

'Did you ever try to find out what happened to your baby?'

'No.'

'You could probably still track her down. It's not too late. I'd give you a hand.'

'No. She's got her own life now. She doesn't need me complicating things.'

'Can I ask my other question, Aunty Lola?'

'You may.'

'Why don't you put the photo in your family book? You could do a special page about your baby and make it look real good. Hey, I know – we could do it together!'

'I've often thought of doing that, Stephen, but I can't. Too many memories. Would you do it for me?'

'Sure! It'll be fun.'

'Then take the photo and keep it safe.'

She gives it to me.

'I'll keep it in my stamp album, Aunty Lola. That always stays in the drawer beside my bed. It'll be really safe there.'

'Good boy. One day – a long time from now, when I'm gone – I want you to have my book. Make the special page for Kathleen Julia then. You won't forget, will you?'

'I won't.'

'I'll remind him,' Mum says.

In a tree outside, birds start singing. The rain's stopped.

'I think we should destroy this fool case now.' Aunty Lola stands. 'I'm relieved it's not going in the garbage – that would have been awful. We'll make a cosy little fire – that's what we'll do.'

When we get outside we see Dad on the back verandah.

'I'm making breakfast,' he calls. 'Who's hungry?'

Aunty Lola touches Mum's arm. 'You go ahead, Rachael. Stephen and I can do this on our own.'

'Are you sure, Lola?'

'Sure as can be.' Aunty Lola looks at me. 'I have a very good helper.'

I follow Aunty Lola to the incinerator. She has the case and a box of matches. I carry a bundle of newspapers.

'Thin strips, Stephen, that's what we want. They'll burn well.'

I tear the paper and let it fall to the bottom of the incinerator. Aunty Lola takes one piece from me and holds a lighted a match to it. When the fire is blazing, she drops in the baby clothes, one at a time. She hangs on to every piece for a few seconds. I don't think she really wants to let them go. But she does. Then she tips in a bundle of letters. I stand on a brick and look into the fire. The letters crinkle up and turn black. Then they're gone.

'At last,' Aunty Lola says. 'At last.'

It's early in the morning and everyone's asleep. I tiptoe past Mum and Dad's room. How can Mum sleep with him beside her? I'd need earplugs. He's a snore machine. Aunty Lola's room is next. Her door's half open.

'Are you awake, Aunty Lola?'

I think she might be going deaf, so I lift my voice up high.

'Are you awake, Aunty Lola?'

'I am now.'

'Can I come in?'

'What in the world for?'

'I can't tell you. It's a surprise.'

'Oh all right. You *may* come in.'

I push the door with my shoulder. The tray clatters and Aunty Lola sits up in bed.

'Now, Stephen. What is this all about?'

'I made you a cup of tea – not too strong – just the way you like it.'

'That's lovely. But why?'

'It's your birthday.'

'No it isn't. My birthday's tomorrow.'

'Really? Are you sure?'

'I think so. It's been held on the same day for eighty years, and that day is tomorrow. You have the wrong day.'

'Aw...Okay.'

Today's the day; the right day. Bright and early, I creep down the hallway past Mum and Dad's room. Dad isn't snoring this time. Mum might have thrown a pillow at him. He told me she does that sometimes. Good thinking, Mum.

I tap on Aunty Lola's door.

No answer.

'Aunty Lola...hellooooo.'

She might be asleep. I'm sure she'd want me to wake her. And I know how to do it.

'Happy birthday to you –'

I sing louder.

'Happy birthday to you –'

And louder.

'Happy birthday, Aunty—'

Aunty Lola opens the door. I've never seen her in her pyjamas before. They're pink. Her slippers are big and fluffy.

'Stephen Kelly, if I could confiscate your voice, I would. I was having a beautiful dream, until you interrupted.'

'But it's your birthday. You're eighty!'

'How kind of you to remind me.'

'If you were playing cricket and you got eighty that would be a really good score. I think you'll probably get a hundred. Don't you?'

'Not if you keep waking me in the middle of the night to sing to me.'

'It's not night-time. It's nearly seven o'clock. In the morning!'

'Exactly what I said – the middle of the night.'

'I made you some toast, but I threw it in the bin. It got burnt because I had to go to the toilet. But there wasn't a fire or anything. Our toaster back home pops, but yours doesn't.'

'That's because it's old, and like all elderly things, it needs its rest. You probably woke it up too early. I'm going back to bed now.'

The door half closes, but then opens again.

'Thank you for the song, Stephen. I think it's the first time anyone has ever sung for me.'

'I know some other songs. Do you want me to sing them?'

'Not just now, dear. Perhaps you'll save them up for when I turn ninety.'

'Okay!'

For the rest of the day I don't mention the birthday. Neither do Mum and Dad. If I was Aunty Lola, I'd be saying heaps. Like, 'Where's my card? Where's my cake? Where are my presents? But she just shuffles about, same as usual, making tea, doing a crossword, falling asleep in her chair…

And then, at two o'clock, the doorbell rings.

Aunty Lola wakes. 'Is someone going to see who that is?'

I'm playing Monopoly with Mum and Dad.

'We can't leave the game right now,' Mum says. 'Would you mind getting it, Lola?'

The doorbell rings again.

Mumbling and grumbling, Aunty Lola shuffles to the door. She comes back holding a bunch of flowers. And she's smiling.

'This is very naughty.' She sniffs the flowers – I hope there are no bees. 'But I must say, they're gorgeous. Daffodils are my favourites.'

All at once we yell, 'Happy birthday!'

'Enough of that. I don't want any fuss. It's simply another day.'

'You're only eighty once.'

'It's just a number, John.'

'But it's a really big number, Aunty Lola!'

Aunty Lola sighs.

Mum takes the flowers. 'I'll pop them into a vase, Lola.'

'No, no, I'll do it.'

'Let me. Please. You're the birthday girl.'

I hear the front gate rattle.

'It's Mr Smith and Allie. And they've got presents!'

'This isn't going to be a party, is it, Rachael?'

'No, Lola. It's just an afternoon tea – to let you know we care about you. You don't mind, do you?'

The doorbell rings. And rings again.

'Hold on!' Aunty Lola calls out. As she plods to the door, she says, 'The birthday girl is on her way.'

'Not bad for a chunk of wood I found on the tip, is it?'

'Hmm…it's very interesting, Norm. What is it supposed to be?'

'Can't you tell, Lola? There's your nose, your mouth…it's the spitting image of you! It's the first thing I've ever carved. I wanted it to be something special. Hope it's all right.'

'Come here, Norm.'

He steps closer.

'I love it.' Aunty Lola kisses him on the forehead.

Mr Smith's face goes bright red, but he looks happy.

'Open mine!' says Allie.

'I will, dear, in time. Goodness me. All this excitement is too much for a country lady of advanced years. I shall need a good lie down at any moment.'

'Open it – please!'

'Very well.' Aunty Lola rips the paper to shreds. 'A scarf. That's exactly what I needed.'

'I didn't know what to get you,' Allie says. 'But Mum said you can never go wrong with a scarf. It's second-hand – I got it at St Vinnie's – does that matter?'

'Not at all. I often shop there myself.'

'What about the colour? Is that all right?'

'Oh yes. The brighter the yellow, the better, I always say.'

'Do you really like it, Miss Webster?'

'Very much, Allie. Very much. Thank you for thinking of me.'

Now it's my turn.

'I didn't get you a present, Aunty Lola, because you said—'

'I said not to, that's right, Stephen, and I'm very glad that you listened to me. You and your mum and dad did all that work around the house, and you bought me a beautiful new heater – that's more than enough presents.'

'But I did do something for you...'

'Oh yes?'

Dad walks in, carrying a cake.

Aunty Lola stares at it. 'What do we have here?'

'I made you a birthday cake! I forget what kind it is – Mum?'

'A chocolate sponge.'

'Aw yeah, that's right. And it's got jam in the middle. Mum helped me, but I did most of it on my own.'

'He did, Lola.'

'I wanted to put candles on it, but Mum said if we lit eighty candles all at once someone might call the fire brigade.'

'Stephen, you don't have to repeat every word I say.'

'Sorry, Mum.'

Aunty Lola smiles.

We sit around the table and Mum gives us party hats. Aunty Lola is the first to put hers on.

'Do I look cool, Stephen?'

'Better than cool,' I say. 'You look sick!'

'Oh...but I feel all right.'

Dad pats her hand. 'Don't worry, Lola. "Sick" means you look great.'

'My, my,' she says. 'It's all so confusing.'

'Have some of my cake, Aunty Lola.'

'Are you a good cook?'

I shrug. 'Don't know. I've never cooked a cake before.'

'You mean you want me taste something that could be horrible – that could poison me?'

I laugh.

'What's so funny?'

'It's not going to poison you, Aunty Lola...I hope.'

'Go on.' Mr Smith cuts a slice of cake and puts it on her plate. 'Be brave.'

'All right then, Norm. If you say so.'

Aunty Lola sinks her teeth into the cake. I watch her every move, hoping so much that she likes it.

'Aarrgh!' She grabs her throat. 'Poison!' She slumps back in the chair. Her arms flop down beside her.

I giggle. So does Allie.

Aunty Lola's eyes pop open. 'You children didn't believe I was poisoned?'

We both shake our heads.

'But you were really funny,' Allie says.

'Well, that's good. I'm glad I still have some use.'

'Do you like the cake, Aunty Lola?'

'It's delicious, Stephen; the cake, the gifts, the friendship – I'm sure I'll never forget any of it.'

Later, Mum and Dad go out and me and Aunty Lola play Scrabble. She doesn't let me make up any words. And I have to spell proper, too. But sometimes she helps me. It's good fun.

I always take a long time to work out what word to put down. Usually Aunty Lola says silly things like, 'I've seen snails move faster,' or, 'I'd like to finish before Christmas, Stephen.' This time she doesn't say anything. I look up and see that she's asleep. She does little whistly snores. And she dribbles a bit too. Doesn't bother me.

Suddenly I remember something.

'Oh nooo!'

She almost falls out of her chair. 'Goodness! What's wrong with you, boy?'

'Your birthday card. I was going to make one for you. I had the paper all ready. I'd even worked out what I was going to say. But I forgot. I'm sorry, Aunty Lola.'

'That's perfectly all right. Perhaps you can send me a card when you get back home. Or better still, a letter. Not any of this twittering or email rubbish; a real letter with some news in it. I'd like to keep up with what you're doing.'

'Sure, but we'll be coming back here. Probably next holidays, Mum said. Then I'll tell you everything that's happened.'

'No, I won't have it. It's such a long way to travel. Besides, I'm certain you have better things to do in your holidays than visit an antique like me.'

'But I want to visit you.'

'Why?'

'Because.'

'Because is not a reason. It's an excuse because you can't think of a reason.'

'Okay...I'll see Allie, too. And Mr Smith.'

'Now that's a reason.'

'I might go fishing again down at the bridge. I'm not sure yet.'

'Well then, if you do come, you'll be a busy lad. I probably won't see much of you, but I'm sure we'll get some time together. We might even fit in a game of bingo.'

'Yeah. I mean yes.'

'Stephen. Perhaps I've been a little too severe with you.' She touches the side of my face. Her hand is warm. 'For the few days you have left here, you may say "yeah" as much as you please.'

'Thanks!'

'You are also permitted to say *can*, instead of *may*.'

'Cool! That is sooo good!'

'But don't let it become a habit when you return home. Is that clear?'

'Um...yeah.'

'Now off you go and let me have some peace. It's been a very long day.'

I don't go.

'Are you waiting for something?'

Aunty Lola puts a hand under her chin. She leans in closer to me, waiting for my answer.

'It's because you're like Blue.'

She makes her eyes go small and squinty.

'Explain yourself, Stephen.'

'That's the reason why I want to come back here.'

'Let me see if I've got this right...you want to visit me because I'm like your dog? Is that what you're saying?'

'Sort of.'

'Do you mean that I have fleas?'

'Noooo!'

'Do I look like a dog? Is that it?'

'No, Aunty Lola!'

'Do you think I have a tail?'

'No way!'

'I'm totally lost. First you name a dead fish after me. Now you compare me to your dog. I feel like I belong in a pet shop!'

'Awww. You know what I mean, Aunty Lola.'

'Hmm...let me take a guess. I know you're fond of Blue, so I suppose being compared to her is possibly a good thing. Is it?'

I nod and nod. 'It's the very best thing!'

Aunty Lola smiles like I've never seen her smile before.

Acknowledgements

I'd like to thank my wife, Dianne Bates. As always, Di assisted me enormously during the writing of this book. Many times I would have given up without her support and encouragement. I'm grateful as well to my writing friends, Chris McTrustry, Vicki Stanton, Maureen Johnson and Sandy Fussell, who guided me along with kindness and sometimes cattle prods (Chris took particular delight in the latter). Thanks also to Beth Norling for her great illustrations, and the Allen & Unwin team of Sophie Splatt and Eva Mills. They've been wonderful to work with. *The Simple Things* has been read and edited by several people, whose advice has helped make it a better book. These clever and generous readers include Sonja Heijn, Jenny Mounfield, Sally Odgers and my outstanding former editor, Leonie Tyle. Last but not least, thanks to my good pal David Gowans, who told me the story about a bird he shot many years ago.

About the author

Bill lives on the south coast of NSW with his wife, the author Dianne Bates. Before writing for children and young adults, Bill worked as a journalist on a suburban newspaper. He has written non-fiction, short stories, poetry and plays. Bill was the winner of the inaugural Prime Minister's Literary Award in 2010 for Young Adult Fiction for his book *Confessions of a Liar, Thief and Failed Sex God.*

Other books by Bill Condon

A Straight Line to My Heart (Allen and Unwin, 2011)
Confessions of a Liar, Thief and Failed Sex God (Woolshed Press, 2009)
Give Me Truth (Woolshed Press, 2008)
Daredevils (UQP, 2007)
No Worries (UQP, 2005)
Dogs (Hodder Headline, 2001)